MOONS OF PALMARES

ZAINAB AMADAHY

Future History Press

ISBN: 10: 1494208466
ISBN-13: 978-1494208462

DEDICATION

To all communities who resist settler colonialism and wanton resource extraction.

CONTENTS

ACKNOWLEDGMENTS

Thank you to Annie Rose Shapero, Nathan Hirstein and Andrew Farris of Future History Press for all your work in making this re-release a reality. Also thanks to Annie Rose Shapero for the beautiful cover design. Finally, thanks to Leith Martin, my middle son, who at the opinionated age of six listened wide-eyed to this story, made incredibly useful suggestions and named one of the characters (guess who).

CHAPTER ONE

The young man pointed his handweapon upward as he crept along the corridor's metallic wall. His grey garment blended in, but his coffee-brown skin and his raven hair, tied at the nape of his neck, ruined his attempt at camouflage. Anyone could spot him and recognize that he should not be in the building.

In an outer office, Major Leith Eaglefeather and two fellow officers watched the slim figure on the holo-imager deftly slip into a shadow-filled doorway as two black-uniformed figures crossed the intersection ahead. It was the last intersection before the weapons storage room, clearly his destination.

What was he up to? Sabotage? Theft? Eaglefeather had no idea, but there were many things he hoped to learn from the intruder. The major and his colleagues watched the figure step out of the shadow of the doorway.

"He should be suspicious," Corporal Pham said, a bemused look on her tan face. "We made it easy enough for him."

The straw-haired Captain Einar Lobo stood next to her. "Just a little further," he urged the figure in the hologram.

The figure suddenly paused and cocked its head, perhaps listening for a noise it could only faintly hear.

"Come on," Captain Lobo whispered anxiously. "Don't get nervous on us. Just a few more metres."

The figure moved on.

Major Eaglefeather felt the tension more than his companions did. The security net was his design. This demonstration would prove its usefulness: by capturing a terrorist, the newly-transferred major would impress his superiors. This was his first posting as chief of security, and making a good impression was important.

The figure glided past the intersection. Two more steps, he thought.

His second step triggered a blinding white light. A split-second later, the figure vaporized.

"Yes!" Corporal Pham declared, her fist shooting triumphantly into the air. "It works, Major!"

"Perfect," Captain Lobo said. "The system is foolproof. He never knew what hit him."

The major felt his cheeks grow warm. Barely able to control his anger, he checked the readings on the computer console behind him. "Who the hell reset these controls?" he bellowed. "I had them on stun."

Corporal Pham's face betrayed her. After a nervous glance at Captain Lobo, she said, "I did, sir. Major Stojic's orders."

"This drill is over. Shut the system down. Now!"

The major fought for control as he strode down the corridor to Major Stojic's office. How dare he! My security system. My drill. He issues an order to reset the controls without consulting me. And now a young man is dead because he broke into the installation. Even if the security net had malfunctioned, the situation had been well under control. True, the intruder's intentions remained unknown, but his only crime was to break and enter. Major Stojic had no right to order his execution for such a petty offense.

By the time he reached Major Stojic's office, Major Eaglefeather was furious. He slammed the door shut, silencing the protesting receptionist on the other side. Major Stojic looked up from his console, his eyes bloodshot but unfazed.

Major Eaglefeather's fists were clenched at his sides. He's not my superior officer. I can blast him to hell, if I want, part of him said. But he's been here for years. He has the colonel's ear. Don't cross him. Not yet.

"Major Eaglefeather," the older major greeted him evenly. "I trust your drill went well."

"Too well. I understand you ordered my people to set the system to deliver a fatal charge."

Major Stojic blinked. "Yes, I did. The colonel is anxious to install the system permanently. I wanted him to see concrete results,"

"Concrete results? Does that mean the intruder had to be killed?"

A tic distorted Major Stojic's face, but his voice remained steady. "Intruders know the risks. He gambled; he lost. Besides, if the system hadn't worked, I doubt he'd be mourning us. Let the terrorists lose a few people and they'll think twice about breaking into secured areas in the future."

The new major took a slow breath. Stojic's from the old school, he reminded himself. If I can reason with him, show him a more effective method ...

"Major Stojic," he began again, "perhaps offering to negotiate with the Menchistas would draw people away from the Kituhwa."

"Yes, well, it's all been tried before." Major Stojic waved his hand dismissively. "We talked that line for years. Frankly, it's hard to tell the Menchistas from the terrorists any more, and this is what it comes down to. I know it's not what you were led to expect when you put in for transfer here, but you'll get used to it."

"I don't think I will, Major. How is this supposed to end if we keep escalating the conflict?"

Major Stojic studied him for a moment and said, "Son, sit down. You and I aren't here to play diplomat. We're here to make sure the Consortium can continue its mining operations. Take my advice and stay out of politics. The colonel won't take to talk of further negotiations with those people."

Although Major Eaglefeather was new to the planet, he knew the old major's attitude was not in keeping with official Terran policy about Palmares. "Those people? You say that as though you think they're different from us. Their ancestors were born on Earth, just like ours."

"Is this your first colonial posting, Major?"

"No. I was stationed on Basilea for two years. Assistant to the chief of security."

"I don't imagine there was much to do there, security-wise anyway."

Major Eaglefeather nodded. "Not any more. The colony is peaceful. The treaty negotiated after the war has held up pretty well. It's just too bad so many lives had to be lost in the process. But it might have been worth it — if we can learn from the mistakes we made on Basilea and not make those mistakes here on Palmares."

"Oh, we have learned, all right. But I think you and I might disagree about what those mistakes were, Major. In any case, it's not for us to decide how to handle the Palmarans. Our orders are from Earth and they are quite clear: keep the quilidon flowing."

"There are better ways of fulfilling those orders."

Major Stojic's eyes narrowed, then he smiled. "Do you know anyone here, Major? Have you been off the base? Seen the compound yet?"

Major Eaglefeather decided not to pursue the matter further, for the moment. Stojic was correct in assuming that he had not seen much of the planet. He had been too anxious to impress Colonel Welch, the base commander, with the new security net he'd been working on since his arrival on Palmares. He had also been fighting off fatigue as his body adjusted to fractionally heavier G-force, lower air pressure and higher temperatures than he had become accustomed to during his two-year stay on Basilea. After a twelve-hour work-day, he had little energy left for sightseeing.

"I haven't had much time off since I arrived," he said.

"Then why don't we continue this conversation tonight? At the Aristide? It's the local live-entertainment centre," Major Stojic said, with a wink. "Virtual reality doesn't compare to the real thing, my boy."

*

That afternoon, as he prepared his report. Major Eaglefeather thought back on the holo-cube he had been required to view before he accepted the posting. Palmares, the narrator had explained, had been the name of a settlement of escaped slaves in nineteenth-century Brazil. There was no explanation of why the colony's founders had chosen the name.

More than ninety percent of Palmares' surface was covered with violet oceans, the narrator had said. Small islands dotted the equatorial region of one hemisphere. Fine red sand beaches lay at the base of spectacularly rugged cliffs, many of which were split by thunderous waterfalls. The only native vegetation to survive terraforming was an inedible blue fungus that thrived in the damp, humid regions.

Palmares' rough beauty was lost on those who originally colonized the planet. Some hundred and seventy years ago, the Consortium, a group of companies that dominated the galaxy's mining industry, had discovered quilidon deposits on one of Palmares' moons. A strategic mineral, quilidon fuelled the machines that space stations and starships used to capture, concentrate, and store energy and was one of the rarest minerals in the galaxy. Palmares' moons contained the largest deposits on record.

Recognizing the sector's potential, the Consortium vigorously recruited labour from Earth and from colonies on Mars, the stations orbiting Venus and the moons around Jupiter and Saturn. Now robots ranging from droids to nanites extracted and refined the quilidon, but live labourers had worked the pits for generations. A job so many light years away from Earth had appealed only to the most desperate. The poorest of the poor, trickling into the sector over several decades, had formed the workforce for Palmares' mining operations. Even today, workers were still needed for day-to-day maintenance and to programme the artificial intelligence that directed the work of the robots.

It wasn't long before the expense of transporting supplies from Earth to the mining station — a journey of seven standard years — became prohibitive. The Consortium soon recognized the cost advantage of developing the then-nameless planet. The Consortium's refinery and workers' quarters on the planet later grew into a settlement and then into a company town.

Originally enclosed under a dome to keep out the carbon dioxide-based atmosphere, the settlement became the major source of supplies for the mining operations. Minerals and metals quarried on the moons were refined on Palmares and used to manufacture basic tools and equipment. Later, foodstuffs for a burgeoning workforce were cultivated under the dome. As the miners' families settled on the planet's surface, a local economy based on the sale of services and consumer goods developed.

Palmares, beyond its role in supplying basic resources to the mining operations, held little interest for the Consortium. The colony's labourers were first to recognize the potential of their new home. Perhaps, speculation held, their impoverished origins permitted them to sever their Terran roots easily. In any case, the workers and their descendants were responsible for engineering Palmares' terraformation. The twenty-five-year project had left the planet just capable of supporting life outside the domed compound. Eventually, the dome fell into disrepair, and today only remnants of it remained.

Meanwhile, a new society had begun to take shape on the planet's surface. Life on Palmares became less centred on the drudgery of the mines and more on building a new society above ground. Perhaps in response to the planet's isolation and its barrenness, Palmarans had become a socially and community-minded people. Ways of life long forgotten on Earth gave meaning to an otherwise routine and lonely existence, or so the anthropologists who studied the planet theorized. Traditional cultures from around the Earth had made Palmares an amalgam as rare as the mineral its citizens mined.

At first the Consortium had supported the changes as complementing its mining activities. Local sources of supply were cheaper than transporting perishables from Earth or maintaining orbiting biospheres. The workforce in the mines seemed happier, more stable, and it grew with every generation.

When the Palmarans asked for home rule, the Consortium did not object, for it suited it to quit supporting the colony. Indeed, it was the Consortium's board of directors which most persuasively lobbied Earth's government to grant Palmares home rule. However, as a quid pro quo, the company had, in several treaties, entrenched its right to maintain a protected base of operations on the planet. That protection consisted of a contingent of Peacekeepers charged with "facilitating Terran interests" and "acting as the liaison between the Terran Government and the Palmaran Governing Council." Most Palmarans had seemed satisfied with the mutually beneficial arrangement. For some, however, home rule would never be enough, and over the last Terran decade, discord had grown louder.

One Palmaran political party, the Menchista, a party enjoying considerable popular support, was now demanding that the Consortium leave Palmares. The holo-cube had noted some of the accomplishments of the twentieth-century Nobel Peace Prize winner, Rigoberta Menchu, whose name the Menchistas had appropriated, then returned to an analysis of the Menchista Party. The Menchistas formed a minority among the elected members of the Governing Council that linked the small communities speckling the planet. The Menchista advocated boycotts, strikes, and other non-violent means of pressuring the Consortium to the negotiating table. Over the past several years, however, factions within the Menchista had become impatient with those tactics. One, calling itself the Kituhwa, after a nineteenth-century Cherokee-traditionalist secret society, had broken away from the Menchista. Kituhwa terrorism and sabotage had become more and more frequent in the last few years, the narrator had said.

Major Eaglefeather's predecessor, a Major Reynolds, had resigned under duress, unable to contain Kituhwa terrorists. On hearing this, Major Eaglefeather had put in for and had been granted a transfer to Palmares, which amounted to a promotion. He had since wondered whether his success had been the result of the impression he'd made in his holo-cubed application or because no one else wanted the post.

The major knew he had yet to grasp the depth of the conflict that gripped Palmares. Nevertheless, he was already forming his own opinions on how to resolve it: keep the Menchista negotiating, maybe even make some concessions. Support for the Kituhwa would dwindle, and soon political isolation would lead to political death.

That, he soon learned, was not the policy option favoured by the Peacekeeper Command. The Consortium was quite willing to negotiate. It was Colonel Welch, who, under threat of withdrawing the Peacekeepers, was holding up the talks. The new major had already convinced many subordinate Peacekeepers that negotiations would be effective, and would minimize blood loss by avoiding armed conflict and the expense of repression. Gaining Major Stojic's trust would be the first step in convincing Colonel Welch, the major had decided, but it was proving to be a difficult task. Perhaps tonight's excursion would change all that.

Technically still inside the compound, the Aristide sat on a small cliff overlooking a red sand beach. Purple waves lapped at the base of the cliff, where the lot for groundskips was full. Gardens filled with tropical foliage imported from Terran hot-houses, their DNA altered to thrive in the alien environment, climbed the Aristide's white-washed clay walls.

The Aristide provided a pleasant respite from the cold grey of Simcoe Base. The tiled red roof, constructed from locally manufactured clay, reminded the major of the architecture he had seen during a short training stint in Latin America. The tiled path up the hill was shaded from the glare and heat of Palmares' powerful sun by tall, manicured bushes. As he neared the top of the path, he peered through the brush at a bright and airy design typical of the terraformed planet. The Aristide's ceiling was high. Four of the six walls had been rolled up on the hexagonal structure's roof, leaving only elaborately carved pillars to guard the wide entrances. Crowded tables filled a shaded patio.

At the top of the path, Major Eaglefeather turned around and looked back. Beyond what remained of the compound wall lay rugged, pebble-strewn terrain and then tumultuous violet seas. Palmares' small but blistering sun had not quite set over the red-streaked islands. On one, he could see the rubble of an old plombonium quarry, surrounded by the ruins of an abandoned Palmaran settlement. Patches of dark green spotted the craggy hills of a more distant island, areas where the industrious Palmarans had cultivated new varieties of vegetation imported from Earth and from other colonized worlds. Marinas, recreational beaches, and untouched gardens of native fungus nestled in the coves and inlets. He turned around. In the distance, in the direction of Tubman, the nearest Palmaran village, there towered a majestic peak. He sighed in appreciation.

Fidgeting impatiently, Major Stojic said, "Not much to look at, is there?"

Major Eaglefeather shook his head. There was plenty to look at, he thought to himself. That the Palmarans could do all this in a century and a half was a testament to their spirit and hard work. He could appreciate that work, and he wondered what kind of a man Major Stojic was that he could not.

Major Eaglefeather felt awkward about coming to the Aristide. The ash left behind when the intruder was vaporised was being tested in the lab, in an attempt to identify him. It seemed cold-blooded to go out and enjoy himself, but he needed to learn more about the Palmaran people, and the Aristide was as good a place as any to begin.

As he followed Major Stojic inside, he caught the aromas of spices lingering in the air. His stomach growled in response. The music was lively but not overwhelmingly loud, for which he was grateful. The dance floor was crowded with people of many colours, shapes, and sizes. Black-uniformed Peacekeepers danced with Palmaran civilians. Other people wore arm patches identifying them as employees of the Consortium's mining operation. Off-worlders, passing through on business or pleasure, completed the crowd.

The hum of conversation in many languages surrounded him. English and Japanese were the official languages of the

Consortium, but it was clear that in the Aristide people freely spoke their own. Major Stojic led him to a table midway from the stage. A hologrammed male head emerged from the table's centre. "Your order please?" it politely asked.

"Cascade," replied Major Stojic, ordering a popular beverage imported from Earth and readily available on most colonies.

"Your order please?" the head asked, turning to Major Eaglefeather.

"Irish ale. Do you have any?"

The head faded briefly, then re-emerged. "It can be synthesized. Anything else?"

"Nothing you could provide," Major Stojic replied dismissively. The head disappeared.

The music faded and applause greeted the group that took the stage. Three men and two women quickly set up percussion instruments at the rear. Their African-influenced costumes featured cowrie jewellery and bright batiked prints. With the room darkened and all attention on the spotlit stage, the drumming commenced. Major Eaglefeather gave in to the reverberating thunder. He was not alone. The crowd moved rhythmically as a brightly-costumed group of barefooted dancers took the stage. Their rapid, synchronized movements were also African in origin. The hips of both the men and the women quivered at speeds he would have thought impossible. Breasts, scarcely covered with colourful halters, bounced provocatively. Dancers and drummers conversed with each other in the classic call-and-response of African music.

"Absolutely primeval, isn't it?" Major Stojic's voice intruded. "The first time I came in here I thought I'd been transported to the nineteenth-century African jungle. One thing about these Palmarans: they know how to have a good time."

Major Eaglefeather hardly noticed when the small mechanized tray arrived at their table. It departed once they had removed their drinks.

The drumming reached a crescendo, then abruptly ceased. The crowd erupted into enthusiastic applause. The majors joined in. The next number featured a solo performance by one of the women. He watched her intently. Her movements were both sensual and athletic. Tight ebony curls whipped around her face and her smile radiated the joy of a playful child. Her skin had both the colour and creamy texture of peanut butter. He was mesmerized by her performance.

"Good, isn't she?" It was Major Stojic again. "That's one difference between Palmaran women and ours. Can you imagine Corporal Pham stripping off and gyrating like that?"

That Major Stojic could use such terms to describe the precisely calculated movements of an accomplished dancer annoyed Major Eaglefeather. Major Stojic had previously confided his belief that Palmaran women were inherently more seductive, more erotic, than their Terran counterparts. Certainly the dance was suggestive, but it implied sexual freedom and joy, which Major Eaglefeather found refreshing.

His stomach growled again. "Do they serve food here?"

"None I would recommend," Major Stojic advised. "Unless you can take strong spices. It's all vegetarian, too, so be forewarned. Palmarans are very superstitious about using animal products."

Allowing his irritation to show, Major Eaglefeather said, "You don't seem to have a lot of respect for these people, Major."

"I respect them. I'm here, aren't I? Appreciating their culture." With a smile, he turned back to the performers. Major Eaglefeather half expected him to start drooling.

The woman ended her dance in a burst of high energy. Sweat gleamed on her hard body as she bowed in thanks to the audience's claps and cheers.

The drumming exploded again and the woman joined the other dancers. Major Eaglefeather was disappointed when they finally left the stage. His eyes followed the muscular soloist all the way off.

"Want to meet her?" Major Stojic asked.

He did. His interest overwhelmed his annoyance at Major Stojic, "You know her?"

"No, but I know the owner," The older major waved his arm.

A statuesque woman who had been chatting with a group of people a few tables away, nodded and strode towards them, her long silver-grey dreadlocks bouncing freely behind her and her flowing yellow dress complementing her cinnamon skin. Her eyes were turquoise and her newly-wrinkled face suggested she was middle-aged — somewhere between seventy and eighty.

"Superb performance, as usual, Nailah."

"Thank you. Major, I'm glad you're enjoying yourself. The next show is at midnight." She spoke in the local English dialect, melodic to Major Eaglefeather's ears. However, something about her expression told him she was working at being friendly to the older major.

“I’d like you to meet a friend — Major Eaglefeather. Our new chief of security."

Nailah’s expression chilled slightly. "Nice to meet you."

“Nailah Aquene," he went on. Then his face lit up. "I think you two have something in common. Didn't you say Aquene is a Cherokee name?"

“Yes, she responded through tight lips. It did not appear she wanted to have anything in common with Major Eaglefeather.

“Who knows? Maybe you're related," Major Stojic laughed. "The major here is completely ignorant about Palmaran culture. That's why I brought him along. He’s particularly interested in that dance your daughter performed. Do you think we can have her join us? Maybe she can explain its origins."

Surely she'll see through that, Major Eaglefeather thought. But she said, “Perhaps,” and signalled to her daughter, who had returned from backstage wearing a purple dress that did little to hide her shapely figure.

Chapter Two

Zaria Aquene studied the faces of the two men looking up at her. Major Stojic she had long disliked, and her mother knew it. So this younger man must be someone important, someone Nailah thought she should meet.

"You remember Major Stojic," her mother said. Zaria nodded in greeting. "And this is his friend, the new chief of security, Major..."

"Eaglefeather. Leith Eaglefeather." The man with chestnut hair and eyes the colour of new sweetgrass offered his hand. His fresh face suggested he, like her, was in his early thirties. "Pleasure to meet you. I enjoyed your performance very much."

Chief of security! No wonder Mother summoned me, she thought. Returning his generous smile, Zaria thanked him.

Major Stojic stood up. "Here, my dear, take my seat. Your mother and I have some business to discuss." He walked off, arm-in-arm with Nailah. The look on the younger major's face as he watched him leave suggested that he was glad to be rid of his company.

"So have you ever been to Palmares before?" Zaria asked, sitting down.

He turned to her and smiled again. "No. It's my first time."

"And not what you expected at all, right?" Zaria had had this conversation many times.

"No. Not really."

He seemed young to be a major and chief of security. "There seems to be a lot of disinformation about our planet. Either that or you Terrans don't take the trouble to learn about us." Punctuated with a smile, the allegation did not offend.

"I suspect it's a little of both."

The shuffle of people on and off the dance floor as the music changed allowed them to suspend their conversation without self-consciousness.

By now they're usually paying me lewd compliments about my dancing or my clothes, Zaria thought. Perhaps this major works slowly. "Do you dance?" she asked, surprised that it was being left to her to keep the conversation going. The major seemed unusually quiet for a Peacekeeper.

"Not since my high school prom. They rented an anti-grav generator, and that was the last time my feet left the ground. But I enjoyed watching you. Were those African dances?"

"Basically. Our troupe is known for mixing different styles. We think it's representative of the diversity of Palmarans. You see, the people who came to this planet generations ago were a mixed bunch. Terran-Jovians, Terran-Martians, Terran-Venusians, Terrans themselves ... They needed a basis of unity — terraforming a planet takes considerable cooperation. They had to forge a common bond from their Terran past, so they revived what they needed from societies out of that past."

"It's fascinating. I don't think any other colony has evolved in quite the same way."

"Well, someone has to preserve the old ways."

"Old isn't always useful, though, is it?"

"No, not at all. But old isn't always obsolete either. We need to take what we can use. In our case, it's whatever lets people be connected — related — to each other. Something besides consumerism and technology."

"Is that how you'd characterize Terran culture today?"

"I'm afraid so."

"You sound like a Menchista."

"Menchista? Me? No, I'm just a dancer."

"You are indeed," he confirmed appreciatively.

She smiled as she got up to leave. "I'm glad you enjoyed the show, Major. Come back again some time."

He looked disappointed at the brevity of their conversation, she reflected on her way backstage. Perhaps, if she saw the major again, she would develop a friendship with him. She might be able to find out what had happened to Rabindra. He hadn't been heard from since he penetrated the Peacekeepers' base. On the other hand, she didn't want to put herself in the position of having to refuse the sexual advances of the chief of security.

Her younger brother, Tariq, and his companion, Persis Nguyen, were at the sound console backstage, setting up the cubes for the holo-musicians who would entertain the patrons until the next performance.

Her brother glanced up. "I haven't seen that major guy around before. Is he new?"

"Straight from Earth, I'd say," Zaria told him. "The new security chief.

"Oh yeah?" Tariq was unimpressed. "Did he hear what happened to the last one?"

Persis studied Zaria intently. “Does he like you?”

"I don't know. Why?"

She shrugged. "Could prove useful. I hope you were nice. He's not too hard on the eyes, is he?"

"Why are you looking?" Tariq demanded in mock anger.

Persis tossed her long raven hair. Her gold-embroidered red tunic brought out the glow of her skin. "I believe your baby brother is jealous, Zaria."

"Back on Earth his type are considered prime meat," Tariq told her. Zaria knew her brother was not really worried. His curly hair, broad shoulders and boyish grin garnered him plenty of attention, male and female.

"We're not on Earth, my love." Persis leaned over and kissed Tariq's cheek, then turned to Zaria. "But, seriously, Zaria. He could be useful to us. He must know what happened to Rabindra."

"Is there still no word from him?" Tariq asked. Rabindra was Persis' second cousin. They weren't particularly close, but Persis shared his family's worry.

Suddenly serious, Persis said, "No, we know he got into the building, but he seems to have disappeared."

"They must have caught him. They're probably interrogating him right now." ,

"I don't think so," Persis said. "In the past they've always announced a capture. The propaganda war and all that. He must be dead. Killed, I should say, and they want to avoid an investigation. That's the only explanation.

"I suppose," Zaria said. She glanced at the major, sipping his beer. Beneath that charming face is a murderer, she thought. No wonder he doesn't say much.

Chapter Three

The crowd that gathered in the square that afternoon did not look at all dangerous, the major noted. It looked ... well, weird. Eaglefeather had never seen anything like it. There were people of all ages, but most were young. Their clothing and hair showed the influence of peoples around Earth and beyond. Some of the younger people had dressed themselves and styled their hair to challenge established Earth norms, and many betrayed more than a casual flirtation with genetic engineering. Strategically-placed fluorescent tattoos, as well as feathers and scales, were clearly en vogue and not restricted to a particular sex or age. There did not appear to be any dominant standard of dress among the roughly three hundred demonstrators.

He watched Captain Lobo climbing the stairs to his post in the clock tower at the square's south end. The captain did not look pleased. He had opposed the issuing of the assembly permit. However, the debate had been closed when no one could find any legal basis for banning the demonstration.

Security had then become the issue, and the major was in the thick of it again. He gave in to Captain Lobo's preference for tight measures, since there was nothing to lose. If there was no trouble, they would simply spend a day in the sunshine, and if trouble came, they would be prepared. He did insist, however, that security personnel stay out of the square, posted in side streets and laneways, out of view. He didn't want to antagonize anyone if he didn't have to.

The preparations had taken up so much of his time and attention that he'd had been unable to follow up on the investigation of Rabindra Woczek, the nineteen-year-old boy vaporised in the security net. All they knew about him — and that thanks to a DNA scan of his ashes — was his name and birthplace, a now-abandoned settlement on a recently-submerged island to the east. A Palmaran comcast had announced the scanty details the major had released about the boy's death. He hoped someone would come forward to claim the nonexistent body. That might give him a lead, but as yet, no one had shown the slightest bit of interest. Now even the major had to consider him less of a priority and concentrate on the business at hand.

Holo-imagers hung suspended over the crowd, ensuring that little would go unrecorded. Many demonstrators looked angry and were shouting that the devices were weapons of some kind. Others suspected their purpose was to record identities for future reference. Their guesses were half-right. Of course their images would be stored on holo-cubes, but the major had also rigged the images to scan for the positronic trigger mechanisms used in the weapons and bombs favoured by the Kituhwa. So far, the scans were negative.

After checking that his troops were in position, the major stationed himself on the square's perimeter, along with ten other Peacekeepers. Two hundred more black-uniformed troops massed out of sight, covering every entrance and exit to the square.

A small screen on the major's wrist control panel displayed what the imagers recorded. With a twist of a small control knob, he could switch from one to another and study both the images and the scanner readings.

The crowd was swelling in anticipation of the keynote speaker.

He tapped a control key on his headset and spoke into the mike. "Captain Lobo, are you in position yet?"

"In position, Major," came the reply. It wasn't necessary for Captain Lobo to be in the tower. Six people had already been stationed there. But the major was worried about the captain. The very idea of the demonstration within the compound had angered him, and the sight of the crowd had outraged him. After hearing Lobo make several derogatory comments loudly enough that the demonstrators could overhear, the major had decided to station him out of earshot.

"How's the view?" he asked, trying to ensure that the captain did not feel slighted by the order.

"Perfect. I can see the whole crowd. There won't be any trouble I can't take out from here." His voice was as chilling and calculating as usual.

"Hold your position. And no firing unless I give the order. With any luck, this will be a peaceful demonstration."

"Yes, sir." The major hoped it was his imagination, but he thought the captain sounded disappointed.

As the major scanned the crowd, he caught himself wondering if Zaria Aquene was there. Now there was a woman who didn't have much use for Terrans. He remembered a passage from a history text he had read long ago. The very idea of race seemed ludicrous now, but it had been very important to the humans of two hundred years ago, even though the characteristics used to classify people by race, and therefore as inherently superior or inferior, had been determined by less than one percent of their genes. Though racism was an anachronism in this century, the same way of thinking was at work in assigning inherent character traits to people of different worlds. It was ridiculous. Not that differences didn't exist. There were differences born of environment and circumstance— intangible and difficult to define, but real all the same — and they were dividing people, making them distrust and even fight each other. He and Zaria Aquene were on opposite sides in a dispute that was born of nothing either could pin down. Absurd, he thought.

The crowd suddenly hushed and the major saw that a groundskip had pulled up. The first person to emerge from it was a diminutive woman, thirtyish, copper-skinned, with long charcoal-coloured hair. Though cl early of mixed ancestry, as were most humans these days, her features suggested her ancestry may have been predominantly indigenous American. Two hundred years ago, they would likely have been allies in the struggle against racism, he reminded himself. In the here and now, however, she was Palmaran and he was Terran and they were, by definition, adversaries.

The woman moved deliberately, glancing around the vehicle, taking in the crowd, her movements suggesting a certain professionalism. She looked up at the clock tower. The major knew she had spotted the Peacekeepers inside. All the same, she looked satisfied and nodded to the passengers inside the groundskip. A tall broad-shouldered man got out, his almond-shaped eyes reading the crowd. Sixto Masika? No, he didn't fit the intelligence reports' description of the young academic and political activist. Two other young men sprang from the skip and began shooing back the crowd. It amused the major to watch them subtly taking their cues from a woman who was barely half their height. Then the man they were awaiting, Sixto Masika, got out, and the demonstrators burst into applause.

Sixto Masika, a thirty-five-year-old tenured professor in Tubman University's Geology Department, had skin the colour of tamarind. Cropped auburn dreads framed his face. His obsidian eyes looked alert. He wore a simple t-shirt and shorts, in contrast to his overdressed bodyguards. In heat that had reached thirty-two degrees Celsius, they sported long pants and lightweight jackets, zipped shut.

As Masika walked to the podium in the centre of the square, the crowd parted respectfully. He nodded to people along the way. Fists waved in greeting. Hands held open in the air received a slap of recognition from Masika or his bodyguards. Comcasters moved in close with their holo-imagers to capture the scene.

Masika's small band of bodyguards reached the podium before him and positioned themselves in a semi-circle. Masika walked into the middle, raised his fists in the air, and the crowd broke into a long, loud cheer.

Using his wrist control, the major manoeuvred one of the holo-imagers to a position above the podium. The almond-eyed man flanking Masika looked up in alarm. The woman raised her hand, signalling him to remain calm.

The major ran his scan. No weapons registered on the holo-imager's sensors. He still had no idea what Masika's bodyguards were hiding beneath their unseasonable clothing.

Several demonstrators began pointing at the holo-imager above Masika's head. Raised fists and angry shouts filled the air.

"They're going crazy, sir!" It was Captain Lobo talking in his ear.

"It's just a lot of noise, Captain. Stay calm." The crowd grew quiet again when the major manoeuvred the holo-imager away from the podium.

The smiling Masika seemed oblivious to the cause of the commotion. He spoke into the microphone hovering before him. "It's good to see so many of us here today."

The crowd cheered again. By now, according to the scanners, close to five hundred people had assembled. The major knew it was not the largest demonstration the Menchista had called, but it was the first inside the compound.

"My friends," Masika continued, "I just returned from the quilombo of Nuevo Xochimilco." Hushed murmurs greeted the news. "The devastation is complete. The volcanic eruption has left only hardened lava in its wake, and unlike volcanic ash on Earth, it is devoid of the nutrients that support plant life. The fields, gardens and homes are all gone, not to be reclaimed in this century."

People in the crowd called out in anger. The major could sympathize to some degree. It was no small feat to cultivate the planet's infertile soil. Removing iron oxides, supplying nutrients and water, and nurturing growth demanded delicate, precise work and the job was not done yet.

Masika continued, his voice strong and self-assured. Clearly, the man was a natural orator, his every pause, intonation and facial expression chosen for effect. "The Consortium claims its mining activities on our moons have nothing to do with this disaster, just as the mining had nothing to do with the quake that killed six people in New Timor last month, or the tsunami that left twelve dead in Martinstown. Terran scientists claim there's not enough evidence to prove that the mining — mining that is eating away huge chunks of the moons that orbit our planet — is destabilizing the tectonic plates beneath us. They're calling for more studies."

The crowd booed.

"There is, I tell you, ample evidence to prove that Palmares is going to break up. It is going to break up because the gravitational force between Palmares and our moons is changing. But the evidence comes from Palmarans, and as far as the Terrans are concerned, Palmaran scientists are not to be believed."

More booing. The major had never heard such charges but doubted there was any truth to them.

"But even if we had not one shred of evidence, even if we had no rationale at all for wanting them off our planet, they would still have no right to be here. No right at all!"

Cheers rang out.

"They abandoned us on this planet. We were cheap labour for the mines. They didn't care how we lived, as long as we showed up for our shifts. Our parents and grandparents sweated and bled to terraform this planet. It was our labour. We made our home here. We raised our children here. By what arrogance do they dare destroy it?"

The cheers grew noisier. Fists beat the air.

"They're getting pretty ugly, Major," Captain Lobo said over the earphones. "I could take a few out."

"Hold your fire, Captain." Major Eaglefeather was getting irritated with him.

"I am a man of peace and reason, my friends." Masika's voice resonated in the square. "But our homes and lives are at stake here. They must respect that. They must respect our right to live, our right to maintain our planet. They have no right to be here. They have no right simply because we say so!"

Some demonstrators began taunting the Peacekeepers nearby. A woman barely out of her teens, with red and green feathers for hair, turned to the major and shouted, "Go home! Go back to Earth! You have no right to be here!" He ignored her but moved away. A chant of "Terrans out" started and gained momentum.

Continuing over the noise, Masika's voice softened. His eyes, even from where the major stood, seemed to moisten. "None of us believes in violence. But anyone could be moved to violence after seeing the devastation at Nuevo Xochimilco. Babies crying from hunger. Elders weak and having no bed to lie in. Refugees. Here, among us, on Palmares. Something those who came before us never imagined could happen!"

At the word "refugees," the chanting reached a crescendo. Either he's very good, or very sincere, the major decided, making another note.

Suddenly he heard the swish of a weapon being discharged. The group around the podium must have heard it too. Two bodyguards moved quickly into action, grabbing Masika and forcing him into a low crouch. Partially covering him with their bodies, they rushed him toward the groundskip.

Simultaneously, the remaining bodyguards, the almond-eyed man and the woman, took small round objects out of their jackets and tossed them haphazardly into the crowd. More weapons discharged.

People ran for cover. Some ripped the sticks from their placards and charged the Peacekeepers. Not knowing what had been thrown into the crowd, the major raised his weapon, set to stun, but he didn't fire. He saw white smoke drifting above the heads of the crowd. Smoke bombs. No wonder his scanners had sensed nothing.

He lost sight of Masika's group. Demonstrators flailed at Peacekeepers in the growing white fog. He could see Peacekeepers firing into the crowd, heightening the panic. Into his headset he yelled, "Everyone hear me now. This is Major Eaglefeather. Hold your fire! I repeat, hold your fire!" But the firing continued, as did the screaming and running.

Blinded by the white haze, a young man with a complex reptilian scale design on his face ran straight into the major, knocking him off balance. The fear in the man's face turned to rage when he recognized the black uniform. He swung his arms wildly, connecting with the side of the major's head. Then he ran off, leaving the major momentarily dazed. Shaking his head to clear it, he shouted into his headset. "Captain Lobo, do you read me?"

"Loud and clear, Major."

The Peacekeepers who had been stationed around the square were advancing now. Their boots clattered loudly on the stone pavement. "Launch a neural paralyzer grenade."

"But sir, we have people down there."

"Do it now! That's an order!"

"Yes, sir!"

The major backed out of the plaza quickly. An instant after the pop of the grenade, he saw the orange flash. The noise abruptly stopped. Bodies froze, then sank heavily to the ground.

Later that evening, it was confirmed that an elderly man had died of a heart attack brought on by the neural paralyser, and six others had been fatally shot. One Peacekeeper had been hospitalized with a broken knee.

There was no sign of Masika. His bodyguards had managed to spirit him to safety. Those who had been stunned by the paralyser would be out for at least twenty hours, so there was no one to question yet.

Captain Lobo and Corporal Pham had been in the tower when the paralyser detonated and so had not been affected. They had watched the events from beginning to end, but claimed they hadn't seen who fired the first shot. The major assigned them to study the holo-cube footage, to try to determine who had fired first.

"Major, sir," Captain Lobo said, "may I speak frankly?" The

major gave a curt nod.

"Well, sir, I really don't think what happened was our fault. That fellow, Masika, was inciting the crowd. Were we supposed to stand there and take all that abuse?"

"You mean you feel justified in disobeying a direct order and firing on unarmed civilians because you disagree with what they say?"

"Excuse me, sir, but we don't know they were unarmed. Maybe they fired first."

"Really, Captain? Well, you had the perfect vantage point. Did you see any Palmarans with weapons?"

"No, sir."

"No," the major repeated after him. "I had the holo-imagers scan the crowd for weapons. Every scan was negative. Under the circumstances, it's reasonable to assume that one of us fired first."

"Yes, sir," Captain Lobo replied, through gritted teeth.

Uneasy with the captain's attitude, the major retreated to his office to study the cubes himself. He didn't find out who fired the first shot, but he did view one segment over and over with great interest.

From the holo-imager's aerial position, he watched as Masika's bodyguards steered him through the crowd just after the first weapon discharged. White haze obscured some of the action, but the sequence was clear. The woman and man who had thrown the smoke bombs caught up with Masika and his bodyguards, then passed them, heading for the groundskip. Then the men shielding Masika stopped abruptly at the sight of something out of the imager's range. The major switched to a cube from another imager and saw what had stopped them.

His weapon drawn and levelled, a nervous young Peacekeeper stood between Masika's party and their groundskip. The woman bodyguard, however, had not altered her course. The Peacekeeper must have seen that she would pass him. But she was so small — how much of a threat could she be? If he allowed her to distract him, the three large men would undoubtedly take advantage. Having viewed the scene repeatedly, the major knew he would have made the same assumptions, would have ignored her in the tension of the moment.

As she pulled up beside the young Peacekeeper, her right foot shot out in a side kick that caught the trooper in the knee. Pain contorted his face as he fell backward. His weapon went off, but in another swift movement the woman used the momentum of his fall to direct its discharge harmlessly into the lavender sky. In the same unbroken motion, her fist lashed straight down and expertly connected with his solar plexus, knocking the wind out of him. Standing over the writhing man, she twisted the weapon from his hand and ran towards the groundskip. Her companions, clearly confident that she could handle the situation, were already piling into the vehicle. The groundskip raced out of imager range a split second later.

He watched, fascinated by the small woman. She acted with the precision of someone who had received expert training. She had deliberately chosen not to kill the Peacekeeper but to incapacitate and disarm him. No doubt she could kill just as cleanly and decisively.

Chapter Four

The female comcaster's face was devoid of emotion as her focus switched from the holo-imager to the screen containing her notes. "Seven demonstrators are now confirmed dead," she read. "One Peacekeeper was wounded. Base commander Colonel Welch denies that his troops fired into the crowd, in a statement this evening he rejected calls for an inquiry and said that hooliganism will not be tolerated. A ban on public demonstrations within the compound walls has been issued..."

Magaly Uxmal switched the broadcast off, and the hologram head faded. She was with Sixto Masika in his small cottage, safe in Tubman Quilombo. Huseni, Rahim and Keoki were on guard outside, making sure that their groundskip had not been followed out of the compound. So far, it appeared it had not.

Masika's residence was no secret, but while the Peacekeepers had never launched an official mission outside of the compound walls, Magaly knew that, unofficially, under Major Reynolds, they had from time to time breached Palmaran home rule to kidnap and murder. She was prepared for any such attempts.

"I don't suppose any comcasters called to ask for your version of what happened?" she said to Sixto. He was still brooding on the couch, one of the few pieces of furniture in his little cottage.

"One did. He asked me why I used my own people as cannon fodder."

She snorted. "An interesting twist of logic. Makes it look like the whole thing was your responsibility."

"Perhaps it was. Maybe holding a demonstration in the middle of the compound wasn't such a good idea."

Shaking her head, Magaly was tempted to tell him not to blame himself. It wasn't that she thought he was to blame. No, just that she doubted anything she said would make a difference. Sixto would feel responsible for the actions of others, even if he weren't at fault. She had never understood that. Never would. Furthermore, she found it annoying. She was outraged at what the Peacekeepers had done. While her rage bolstered her commitment to driving the Terrans out, Sixto's guilt left him paralysed. He was too sensitive for the work that had to be done. Sooner or later he would realize that and leave the job to her. For now, however, he had his role. He inspired people, motivated them, made them imagine something better. And once convinced, they lined up to join the Kituhwa and fight.

Something was moving outside the door. Magaly reached for her handweapon and crouched low, behind the couch. Masika, less wary, stood up. "Get down!" she commanded. He joined her behind the couch.

"Who's there?" Sixto called out.

"It's me!" a familiar female voice replied. Magaly holstered her weapon and opened the door.

Zaria Aquene stepped inside. She hugged Magaly briefly and then turned to Sixto. Sighing, she wrapped her arms around his neck and pressed herself against him in a tight embrace.

"How did you get out of the compound?" Magaly asked when they stepped apart. "I heard there was a curfew."

"There is."

"You mustn't risk your life foolishly, Zaria," Sixto admonished her.

"I had to know you were all right."

"I'm fine. Just fine." They embraced again.

"I'll be leaving now," Magaly announced, rolling her eyes. "See you in the morning, Sixto, Zaria."

Once Magaly had left, Zaria turned to the man she loved. "What the hell happened today?"

He frowned. "What happened? They fired on us!"

"Why? Did you give them any reason?"

"How can you ask me that?" He looked wounded.

"I'm sorry. It's just that that's never happened before. They've never fired on people who were clearly unarmed."

"Not according to the comcast. The official line is that we fired first."

"That's ridiculous," she snapped. "Seven people died. Not one of them was a Peacekeeper. How did you escape?"

"We got away in the confusion." He collapsed on the couch and let his head fall into his hands. "I can't shake the feeling that all this is my fault."

"It's not. We have every right to hold a demonstration. Every right to be there. None of us had any reason to believe the Peacekeepers would fire on unarmed civilians."

He studied her for a moment, then spoke. "Magaly thinks it was an attempt to assassinate me."

"She could be right. There's a new Terran security chief, just transferred here. Major Eaglefeather. It might have been his doing."

"This is important information. How did you come by it?"

"He came into the Aristide last night and introduced himself."

"Then you know him?"

"We're acquainted."

Raising an eyebrow, Sixto asked, "Could you get better acquainted?"

She frowned. "What are you asking me?"

He held his hand out in a gesture of protest. "Not that. Just be friendly with I him. Enough to get him to reveal things. Information. Anything might be significant these days."

It had been done before. Tariq and Persis were good at it. So good it had never been necessary for Zaria to try. "I won't sleep with him," she said.

"I would never expect that."

She drew him to her and stroked his hair. It was the way they usually began a night of lovemaking.

Chapter Five

Major Eaglefeather waited expectantly. Aside from the orientation interview upon his arrival and the weekly meetings of the senior officers under the colonel's command, he'd had little occasion to talk to Colonel Welch. The colonel was businesslike and efficient. At staff meetings he seemed perfectly reasonable, a man who listened to a range of opinions before making a decision.

At the colonel's invitation, the major seated himself. The colonel was in excellent shape for a middle-aged man. His mixed ancestry had given him unusual and interesting features. Clean-cut and expertly coiffed, he could have passed for a Consortium executive, had he not been wearing Peacekeeper black. Like a cocktail party host, he mixed drinks for the major and himself, then sat at his console.

"I asked you here to congratulate you on your work with us. So far," the colonel began.

The major was mildly surprised. Major Stojic had led him to think that the colonel wasn't the least bit impressed with his work.

"Congratulate me?"

"Absolutely. I understand your new security net is online and functioning efficiently. With the trouble we're likely to see in the days ahead, we're going to need it."

"Perhaps not, Colonel. I still believe in its deterrent effect."

"Yes, I understand from Major Stojic that you would prefer to have the system set to stun."

"That's correct, sir." He leaned forward, glad for the

opportunity to put his ideas directly to the colonel. "I think it would discourage entry just as effectively as a fatal charge."

"I disagree. You don't know how many times we have taken these terrorists into custody only to be sorry for it later. Prison riots, escape attempts, rescue missions."

"Well, if the system is to remain set to kill, maybe we can post some sort of warning," the major persisted. "Announcements over the comnet that the system is in place. To back them off."

The colonel leaned back in his plush chair "Why?"

"In training they always tell us that nothing is impregnable. Sooner or later, someone is going to beat any security system. Despite the most advanced technology, the human factor cannot be controlled. Security is in part a psychological game, and a good security system is designed to discourage entry in the first place ..."

"Yes, yes," the colonel interrupted with a wave of his hand. "Well, I don't think much will discourage the fanatics I've seen on this rock. They don't think logically like you and me. No, they can be quite irrational. You saw that fellow in the square today, Sixto Masika? The one who incited the riot? He's quite typical. Can't be reasoned with."

"Have you tried?"

The question appeared to surprise the colonel, possibly because it was not the major's place to ask it, but the colonel must have been in a generous mood.

"My predecessor did. He was reassigned. Transferred in disgrace. He kept making concessions to the Palmarans. They wanted aid for reclaiming lands lost to volcanic and quake activity. They got it, but they weren't satisfied. They won't be satisfied until we pack up and go home. That is what they ultimately want, you see. And that is quite impossible."

"Is there any truth to the claim that mining the moons is affecting the planet?"

The colonel looked annoyed. "The planet is geologically unstable. They knew that when they settled here, but they kept coming. The Consortium provided them with equipment, technology and monetary assistance to terraform this planet. Now that they've done it, they want us off. And you can bet that if we leave, they'll take over the mines the next day. That would spell disaster for Earth. We cannot relinquish control over the largest source of quilidon ever discovered. Can you imagine what it would be like? Being dependent on the rabble here to supply us with an essential energy requirement?"

"Has anyone researched their claims? Looked at their evidence?"

"It's been done. Major." His tone was curt. "Their findings cannot be duplicated. It's difficult to accept that natural disasters can still occur. People lose their lives, and it's easier to blame the Consortium — that way the Palmarans don't have to take any responsibility for the mess they've created down here. They find some scapegoat, instead of instituting population and environmental controls."

"I see. But the Palmarans seem quite convinced."

"Yes, well, they have that madman Masika whipping them into a frenzy on a regular basis."

"Perhaps if we showed some good faith we could win away some of Masika's support?"

"What kind of good faith?"

"A warning about the security system, to start with."

The colonel paused to consider. Then he broke into a tight smile. "All right, Major. Post your warnings. See if it makes any difference."

He seemed so confident it would make no difference that the major wondered if he might be right. "Thank you, sir."

Chapter Six

Just before Zaria took the stage for her first performance of the night, she saw the new major seated at a table near the back. She was glad she hadn't spoken to him earlier. She needed more time to think about how to approach him, how to cultivate his interest and trust while maintaining her distance. She had no intention of winding up in his bed just to get information, but she felt ill-prepared. Her training had not prepared her to deal with such situations and she lacked experience with men. Sixto Masika was one of the very few men she'd been intimate with. She was the daughter of a woman thought to be a collaborator, and Palmaran men often treated her as if she carried a plague. Terran men found her interesting, but she had no interest in them.

Her mother, Nailah Aquene, had been a covert operative for the Menchista for years. For her, the issue was clear: independence from Earth and Palmaran control of the mines. Nailah had never given the Peacekeepers the slightest reason to believe she was an agent for the Menchista. Word had it she was even married to a Terran, though he was never seen at the Aristide. Throughout her childhood, Zaria and her brother had been taunted at school and shunned by other young Palmarans and had learned to make do with a small circle of friends whose parents were in the Menchista.

On the day home rule was granted to Palmares, Zaria had rushed home from school, almost faint in her joy that the truth would finally come out. But her mother didn't join in the celebrations. Nailah was not yet willing to shed her cloak.

"The Consortium and the Peacekeepers will remain here," Nailah had explained to her daughter that night. "They are a powerful alliance with no concern whatsoever for our people. Their profit-making will always conflict with our needs. One day, we'll be ready to act. I want to make sure I'm in a position to help when that day comes."

When the Kituhwa split from the Menchista, Nailah went with them. The Aristide became a Kituhwa intelligence post. Zaria and Tariq had themselves become full-fledged Kituhwa.

The beating drums called Zaria to centre stage. She began to dance and was well into her performance when a man rose up from his seat and stepped towards the stage. The weapon he held was trained on her. She froze.

A scream cut through the music. The drums stopped. Shinichi, a frail young man she barely knew, stood before her, his face pale and contorted with hatred. "Traitors! Collaborators! You make a mockery of our culture." His puffy, red eyes darted from her to the room and back.

From the corner of her eye, Zaria saw her mother coming from stage left. Nailah stepped between her daughter and Shinichi. "Easy, Shinichi. You don't want to hurt anyone with that."

"Filthy traitors!" Shinichi screamed. "My partner died in the square yesterday! We're trying to get these bastards off Palmares, and you — you welcome them. You have them here every night, entertaining them, fucking them, selling us out!" Tears began to roll down his face.

Still shaking, Shinichi half turned toward the audience, his weapon now on Nailah. "You Palmarans out there," Shinichi shouted. "I'm talking to you! How can you do this? You sit here drinking and laughing with them, having a good time, while my children ask me why their mother is never coming home."

"Shinichi." At the sound of Nailah's voice, he focused on her again. "We're very sorry about your partner, but we don't want anyone hurt here tonight," she said softly. "Please put your weapon away and go home to your children." Then her gaze fixed on something behind him. He spun around to see Eaglefeather only steps from his back.

The major froze as Shinichi's weapon levelled on him. "Just put the weapon down, sir. I'm sure you don't want to shoot anyone."

"Not as much as I want to shoot you."

"And that is just the point. These people are not your enemy. You're angry at the Peacekeepers. With very good reason."

"I should shoot you here and now. Give you as much of a chance as you gave my partner." Shinichi's hand shook violently.

"You could do that," the major said, "but there are dozens of Peacekeepers in here. If you shoot me or anyone else, they'll shoot you dead. And your children will lose another parent. Give me your weapon. You can walk out of here and go home to your kids."

Shinichi looked down at the weapon in his hand. "And what about my partner?" he asked weakly. "Who's going to pay for her death?"

"I don't know, but I give you my word I'll try to bring her killer to justice."

Slowly, hands trembling, Shinichi reached out and dropped his weapon into the major's outstretched palm. Black-uniformed Peacekeepers surrounded Shinichi, grabbed his arms and twisted them behind his back. He winced in pain. Zaria was about to protest, but the major spoke quickly. "Let him go!"

"But, Major..." one of them began to argue.

"Let him go!" the major ordered firmly. "We've caused him enough grief."

Reluctantly, the Peacekeepers relinquished their grip. Tariq came to Shinichi's side, placed an arm around the shorter man's shoulder and led him out of the Aristide. The major handed one of his men the weapon and said something Zaria couldn't hear.

"That's all for this show," Nailah announced. Some laughter indicated the tension was dissipating. "The next live show is at midnight. For now, we have holo-music for your enjoyment." The noise returned to normal. Persis stepped backstage to insert a music cube.

Nailah strode up to the major, with Zaria behind her "Thank you. Major. If not for your intervention, that might have ended in tragedy."

"Yes," he agreed, "but I have to say that I'm impressed by your courage."

"A mother can be very courageous when her children's lives are at stake, Major. Have you eaten yet? Perhaps a meal at my expense? To express my gratitude."

"It's not necessary."

"Please, I insist."

He smiled at Zaria. "Perhaps you'd care to join me."

"Yes, I'd like that." His smile made her think of a young boy asking for his first date.

"My table is over there."

Zaria turned back to see her mother looking on serenely as he led her to his table. After they'd ordered meals from the holo-head, she studied him curiously.

"Well, Major Eaglefeather, I'm very impressed with the way you handled that — no bravado, no threats, no intimidation. I've never met a Peacekeeper who actually kept the peace. I don't believe many of your colleagues would have handled the situation quite like that."

"There's been enough bloodshed. And please, call me Leith."

"I thought Leith was short for Lethal. Apparently not."

He grinned. "I hope not."

"Why did you let him go?"

"His kids are going to need him."

"And you don't think he'll be back tomorrow?"

The major shook his head. "No, he doesn't strike me as a killer. I don't think he'll be back."

"Is it true what you said? Do you intend to look for the Peacekeepers who fired on the crowd yesterday?" She remembered the earnest look she'd seen on his face when he had made that promise to Shinichi, but she had her doubts.

"I've already started looking."

"Does Colonel Welch agree?"

He made a vague gesture. "Not really. No, the Colonel is going to be a problem."

Surprised that he would answer frankly, Zaria decided that, for now, there was no sense pressing the point. "Were you stationed on Earth before coming here?"

"No, I spent two years on Basilea, as assistant chief of security."

"Don't take offense, but you don't act like your typical security chief. What made you choose that line of work?"

Her comment annoyed him, she could tell, but he kept his tone courteous. "I'll take that as a compliment, but you shouldn't generalize about security chiefs, you know."

"I'm afraid my generalizations are based on experience."

"I can understand that. But we're not all alike. I subscribe to the belief that law enforcement officers — especially Peacekeepers — should be mediators. People turn to violence because they can't find other means or don't see other options. We should be trained to help resolve differences peacefully."

"Well, that all sounds very nice, but..."

"Yes?"

"It's also a little naive."

He nodded, "I suppose it does sound that way."

"And anyway, you don't strike me as a soldier."

"I'm not a soldier. I'm a Peacekeeper."

She made her voice light. "Whatever you call yourself, you're different from your comrades. Surely you've noticed?"

He leaned back in his chair and studied her for a moment. "While I was at the Peacekeepers' Institute on Earth many years ago, I fell in love with a woman. We were engaged to be married. I don't recall a time when I was happier. We had great plans for the future, but she was keeping this terrible secret. At least it was terrible to her."

"What was that?" Zaria asked, after an appropriate pause.

"She was Martian."

Zaria knew that humans of Martian birth were a rarity on Earth. The low gravity on Mars allowed them to grow tall and thin but not to develop the density of muscle and bone tissue necessary for worlds with higher gravity. Months of intensive hormone therapy, with unpleasant side effects, were needed for them to build the tissue mass that would allow them to function normally in Terran gravity.

"She had hidden that fact from me for a year. When I found out it was by accident. She usually got up very early in the morning, you see, then teased me for sleeping in. One day I was going to surprise her by joining her for breakfast. Instead, I found her viewing p-mail messages from Mars, sent by her family. I caught enough to understand that she hadn't grown up on Earth. She was livid, humiliated. There was a terrible scene — I'll spare you the details — but it was like she'd suddenly become a stranger. She couldn't bear for me to know she was Martian. She called the wedding off and never spoke to me again."

"Incredible self-hatred."

"Yes, it was. And when I got over my anger it made me think a lot about this — this worldism that so many people subscribe to these days. How crazy it is. What it does to people. And I started to ask myself whether I would have gotten involved with her if I had known from the beginning. I'm ashamed to admit that I probably wouldn't have."

"That's a pretty harsh thing to admit about yourself."

"It was good in a way. I haven't been the same since, that's for sure, and I'm glad about that."

"So am I." Zaria reminded herself that whatever he called himself, he was still a soldier. She leaned back in her chair, putting an appropriate distance between them. "You seem young for a major."

He shrugged. "I may be young, but I'm ambitious."

"Really? How so?"

"Yes, really. I'll accept posts that no one else wants. It's been good for my career, so far."

"I see. Where on Earth are you from?"

"Canada. A small town outside of Toronto."

"Do you miss it? All that snow?"

"It's not all snow. But, no, I can't say that I miss it much. And you? Where are you from?"

"Palmares, of course."

"Yes, but where?"

"Sorry, but I don't often get asked that question. Terrans rarely know the difference between one quilombo and another. I'm from Tubman, on the mountain plateau on the far side of the island. I was born there."

"You must have a spectacular view from up there. Perhaps you'll invite me up some time."

"It's a date."

"What does key-lom ...?"

"Quilombo?" She spelled it for him.

"Quilombo," he repeated. "I've heard the word. What does it mean?"

"It means a town or a village. The word originated in Brazil, in slavery times. African slaves escaped from the plantations on the coast and fled to the interior where they set up free settlements they called quilombos. They had families, grew their own food ... Many quilombos survived for years. But the slave masters couldn't leave them in peace and many Africans died defending their quilombos. The unlucky ones were dragged back into slavery. The original colonists on Palmares chose quilombo over village, town, city, whatever."

"Fascinating. I never knew that."

A mechanized tray appeared beside the table. It waited obligingly as they removed their plates of food and then rolled away. The major sniffed at his plate, then examined it carefully.

"Look good?" asked Zaria.

"It looks fine, thanks." He ventured a bite, chewed and swallowed. "Good," he mumbled, and took more. "Zaria," he said between mouthfuls, "where do you stand in all this? Do you think the mining operations on the moons are destabilizing the planet?

Many of your people seem to think so."

Assuming what she hoped was an air of indifference, she said, "I've heard conflicting evidence, and both sides have a vested interest in holding the positions that they do. I don't know what to think."

"You have no opinion?"

"I'm a dancer. I stay out of politics. Why don't you tell me what you think?"

"I think we better find out. If the Consortium is wrong, the damage to Palmares will soon be irreparable. In fact, I think mining operations should be suspended until there is no doubt."

"Palmarans have been shot for saying such things. I'd keep my opinion to myself if I were you. You might get transferred out."

"I'd rather leave the Forces if I can't do what I was sent here to do in the first place: keep the peace."

She chewed for a moment before speaking again. "Look, I don't mean to offend you or anything, but you have a real hero complex."

"A what?" He laughed, but looked uncomfortable.

"You, fresh from Basilea, arrive on Palmares, a world you know nothing about, to single-handedly mediate a war? Thanks anyway, but we don't need a saviour."

"I didn't mean to suggest that I could single-handedly do anything —"

"No, but you are naive. The Consortium will never voluntarily pick up and leave — not until the quilidon runs out and even if we lose Palmares in the process."

"You sound like a cynic," he told her. "I prefer to have hope."

"Quilidon is essential in maintaining Earth's standard of living. It provides you Terrans with the ability to capture and store energy. It allows you to travel through the galaxy quickly and efficiently, conquering and colonizing, securing scarce raw materials to sell back home. Hope all you want. But a lot more blood will be shed before this is over."

Nailah came striding towards them. The anger in her mother's face made Zaria see the mistake she had made. Unable to hold her feelings in check, she'd allowed the conversation to deteriorate. Instead of cultivating the major's interest and trust, she had antagonized him.

"Zaria," her mother said, her lips drawn tight. "You have a costume change before the next show, don't you?"

"Yes, I do. Excuse me, Major."

"Sorry, Major," she heard Nailah say as she walked away, "perhaps she can join you later. Is your meal satisfactory?"

Backstage, Zaria waited for her mother. "What were you thinking?" the older woman demanded.

"Eavesdropping through the headwaiter, Mom? You haven't done that since my first date."

"You've never been mixed up with the chief of security before. You were supposed to be friendly, gain his confidence, not get yourself put on the death list. You said too much about what you really think, Zaria."

"I was just being myself."

"Don't. It can get you killed."

Zaria collapsed on a couch. "I guess I blew it."

"Maybe not completely." Her mother absently picked up a costume and folded it. "You can still win his confidence, through a carefully staged incident."

"Mother, is it really worth it? Is he really that useful?"

Nailah frowned. "Is he getting to you?"

Zaria considered the question. The major might not be your average Peacekeeper, but he was keeping the Consortium's peace. Remember the demonstration in the square, she told herself. Seven dead, all Palmarans, and he was in charge.

Zaria swallowed. "No. He's not getting to me, not exactly. It's just — I don't know. He's inconsistent! You heard him. He seems more naive than dangerous. Rabindra is dead. We know that. And probably on the order of that man. Yet he treated Shinichi with such compassion."

"He had an audience when he was with Shinichi."

"Does that explain it?"

Her mother softened. "No, perhaps not. People are

inconsistent, Zaria. Sometimes we are living contradictions. Torturers who commit the most brutal acts can go home and, like any loving parent, tuck their children into bed. But does that mean they should not be accountable for their crimes?"

"No, of course not. But what if we're wrong about him? What if he's sincere?"

"Perhaps the major is not what he appears to be at all. My first impressions about your father were certainly wrong. But it was your father who proved me wrong — I was not about to risk my life to test his sincerity, and you shouldn't take any risks with the major. If he's everything he seems to be, you're in no danger. On the other hand, if he's manipulating you, or creating false impressions, for whatever purpose, you had better beat him at his game. Or you won't live to speculate."

"Makes sense," Zaria had to admit.

"Good. Now, get your brother in here. I have a plan."

Chapter Seven

At first, Major Eaglefeather was angry. Saviour, indeed! He didn't deserve that. She didn't listen to me, never gave me a chance to explain. Then the performance started. It was a new dance, what he thought of as Hawaiian: grass skirts, frangipane leis and sea shells, scantily-clad men and women. Zaria mesmerized him again.

His mood mellowed. I guess I hurt her feelings, just when she was beginning to like me. He thought about her smile, her laughter. She'd certainly asked him a lot of questions, personal questions.

As she danced, he imagined her coming to his table after her performance. They would apologize to each other. She would lean over and kiss him lightly. Then, unable to contain her passion, she would suddenly kiss him hungrily, ask him to her bed, and he would feel her strong muscles melt into his body.

Major Stojic sat down next to him, uninvited. Eaglefeather listened passively to Stojic's comments on the latest comcast about the demonstration and left as soon as the performance was over.

He walked down the stone steps behind the Aristide and turned toward the red sand beach. The weather was pleasantly warm. A high degree of climate control was one of the advantages of terraformed colonies. Palmares' environmental control system rarely allowed extremes of temperature or humidity. Rain, if it were needed, was engineered to fall at night, but the comcasts said tonight would be clear.

The two white moons shining brightly in the violet sky reminded him that he still had a lot to get used to on this world. Palmares had never really known darkness. At least two of its three moons always shone at night. Even through cloud cover, their reflection of the sun's sharp white light made Palmaran nights dim rather than black. The major missed being able to see stars. Squinting, he studied the quarries, large dark splotches on the white surfaces of the moons. The third moon, visible during the day, would look the same.

Hoping to free his mind of Zaria, he went over his conversation with Colonel Welch. How much of what the colonel had said was true, he would have to wait to find out. After a while, the relentless waves lapping at the shoreline brought back memories of Canada's rugged east coast, but when he looked out over the Palmaran ocean he was struck by the contrast.

Virtually devoid of life, the sea was crystal clear except for stirred-up sand. The water got its purplish tint from iron oxide and blue fungi lining the ocean floor. Palmaran soil had to be specially treated, impregnated with microorganisms, before it could support vegetation. Composting was almost a religion among the Palmarans.

The sharp sound of footsteps descending from the cliff above him made him stop short. Three large men were climbing down the cliff's stone steps. They fanned out, one heading straight for him, another for the beach ahead, the third moving behind him. To his right was the cliff, to his left, the sea. He was armed but assumed his assailants were too.

He recognized them as Sixto Masika's three male bodyguards. His mind raced as they ran toward him. Now two blocked his way. Almond Eyes, much larger than he had looked earlier, stayed behind. Their stomachs were flat and hard and if the small woman on the imager clips of the demonstration had been any indication, they were well-trained.

The shortest of the three, half a head taller than the major, spoke first. "I understand you're the new security chief. So what happened in the square the other day must have been your doing." His thin nose and chin seemed to emphasize his no-nonsense delivery.

The major wondered how he should respond. Aggressively? Sympathetically? Defensively? Did it matter? He was about to warn them that he was armed, when he was distracted by the sound of rocks tumbling from the cliff. He made out two figures, half sliding, half running down the cliff.

"Leave him!" He heard Zaria call from the distance. Now he could see that the other, a man, was one of the percussionists in the dance troupe. By the looks of him, he was a close relative of hers.

Thin Nose fidgeted and exchanged glances with his comrades. The major felt doubly uneasy — worried for Zaria's safety as well as for his own.

The drummer reached them several steps ahead of Zaria. It was the man who had led Shinichi out of the Aristide. "Move along, guys," he urged, only slightly out of breath. Apparently drumming was a good way to stay fit. The drummer, not a small man either, stepped between the major and the two men before him.

Thin Nose spoke again, this time a little nervously. "You collaborators should go back inside and pretend you see nothing. As usual."

"We aren't leaving," the drummer replied. His voice was firm. "You'd better go." By now Zaria was standing just behind the drummer. She, too, was panting only slightly.

"Get out of here before you get hurt." This came from the man behind them.

"I might not be the only one to get hurt tonight," the drummer said matter of factly. "Three against one are comfortable odds. Three against two changes matters."

"Three against three," Zaria corrected him. The major doubted Zaria would be much use in a fight. Then he remembered the small woman at the rally again and realized there was no telling what Zaria might be capable of.

"You'd defend him?" said Almond Eyes incredulously, pointing at the major.

"The major is our guest," said the drummer.

Thin Nose spat at the ground, just missing the major's boot. He jerked his head at the others. "Let's go," he said. "There'll be other times. And we'll deal with those two later."

They swaggered slowly down the beach, like teenaged toughs walking away from a fight while trying to project the illusion that they were doing their opponents a large favour. When they were out of earshot the major thanked the drummer. "Hey. We're even," the drummer said. "Earlier this evening I was looking down the barrel of a gun, remember? We haven't met yet. I'm Tariq."

"My brother," Zaria said, as the men nodded formally at one another — the Palmaran custom when being introduced. "Rahim, the guy behind you, was in the Aristide tonight and left just after you did. The way he was watching you made me suspicious. Then when I saw him meet up with Keoki and Huseni, I figured they were up to no good, so I got Tariq and we chased after them."

"You know them?"

"We've seen them around," Tariq said. "They don't come into the compound much and they've never come to the Aristide until tonight. They're friends of Sixto Masika, close friends. As you can imagine, they don't hold us in high esteem."

"Major," Zaria interrupted, "after what happened in the compound yesterday, I don't think it's such a good idea for you to be wandering around isolated places at night, not while tempers are running so high."

"I suppose you're right. I guess it never occurred to me that something like this might happen. At my last posting, crime was virtually nonexistent. Just the occasional night-time mugging. Of course, this would be considered broad daylight on Basilea."

Zaria smiled. "Do you have a groundskip to get you back to your base?"

"No, but I can hitch a ride with Major Stojic," he said, though he didn't want to leave.

They accompanied him back up the cliff. "Tell me, Major,"

Tariq asked him as they climbed, "why is Basilea so free of crime?"

"Circumstance as much as anything," said the major, grunting a little as he headed up toward the Aristide. "A thick ring of rock and ice surrounds the planet, shielding it from the light and heat of its sun. In spite of its relative proximity to a class G star Basilea is extremely cold — and its atmosphere, though rich in oxygen, is much too thin to support human life. So colonists live within domes of translumium four centimetres thick, totally dependent on the technology that controls the domes. Weapons aren't permitted, of course, for fear that a stray shot would pierce a dome, and almost everyone's movements are tracked — safer for them and for the planet. So, as you can imagine, under the circumstances, criminal behaviour is difficult and —"

"The legacy of a failed uprising," Zaria cut in.

"Excuse me?"

"After a colonial rebellion on Basilea was quashed some thirty years ago, the Peacekeepers there decided that closer monitoring and stricter control over the population would prevent any future insurrection. They've been right so far."

"I was stationed on Basilea for two years," the major retorted. "It's been my experience that the Peacekeepers, the Consortium and the local government work well with each other. Political disagreements are worked out amicably. It's a model which might be useful here on Palmares."

Zaria raised an eyebrow. Her brother nudged her slightly, and she said nothing more till they reached the Aristide where she bade the major good night. "I hope," she said, "that what happened tonight won't keep you away from the Aristide."

Chapter Eight

“That's crap!" Magaly said, gesturing angrily "It wasn't Gandhi's philosophy that won India's independence. It was the cost of maintaining the colony. If the Indian people had chosen to fight, a lot more of them would have survived to see Independence Day."

"Ridiculous," Sixto rebutted, his voice calm. "I don't usually talk about what might have been, but had they done it your way, even more people would have died. Violence only breeds more violence."

"Well, we're not going to convince the Terrans to leave by turning the other cheek." She paced agitatedly.

"I'm not suggesting we adopt Gandhi's strategies, just that we avoid bloodshed, keep our targets non-human." He sat calmly on the couch, one leg crossed over his thigh.

"And when they retaliate by killing Palmarans, we ignore it? I don't think so."

It was an old argument. Sixto had expressed his admiration for Gandhi's philosophy, part of which he said required you to die rather than take another's life. His comments had set Magaly off. Had they not been waiting for Tariq, she would have left the cottage in disgust. Her patience with Sixto's strategy had reached its limits, and since the loss of Rabindra, one of their best operatives, she had been eager to retaliate. The incident at the rally had made her even more so. Tariq's vidphone message had left her restless and irritable.

Tariq finally arrived, Zaria in tow. Now they could get to work. After quick hugs all around, he pulled out the ignition code card that Magaly had been waiting for. His transmission earlier in the day had left out the details. She began to question him.

"How did you get it?"

"Two Consortium pilots came in the Aristide tonight. They were so wasted on Bliss that they never noticed when I lifted their ignition cards and copied the magnetic signal." He handed her a thin flat oblong.

Magaly persisted. Had anyone seen him take it? Copy it? Put it back? Who knew he had made a copy? Finally, she exhaled loudly and declared, "Perfect. Absolutely perfect, just what we need."

Zaria was already seated at Sixto's computer console, tapping keys. "All we have to do is break into the navigational system."

"Yes," Sixto agreed. "But our calculations will have to be exact."

"As will our timing," Zaria added, adjusting the goggles that would let her view the files in the navigational computer she was about to hack into.

"No problem," Tariq assured them. "O-nine-hundred tomorrow. That's when the barge docks. Did I mention I was eavesdropping on their conversation?"

"That's a bad habit," Zaria teased him.

"Hey, what can I say," he grinned. "I'm not as well-mannered as you."

Zaria gained access in only a few minutes and began to upload the data into the helm control system. She worked with more accuracy than speed. It was close to dawn by the time she finished.

It was a routine morning for Yumiko Kapoor, director of operations at the Consortium's orbiting refinery. Two automated barges had already docked, offloaded several tons of raw quilidon and departed for Samora Moon to reload. A third, from

Kanesetake Moon, was on its way.

Kapoor joined the two techs on duty in docking control. The triangular chamber had two seats facing the consoles that lined one wall. It was a cramped, dimly lit space, and usually held only the two workers needed to pressurize and depressurize the docking bay as auto-piloted barges came and went with their cargo.

Yumiko Kapoor didn't need to be there for routine docking and unloading. It was unusual for her to be anywhere near docking control, but one of the techs was new to the post and the other had just received a poor performance review. Otherwise, Kapoor would have been in her office, revising the station's budget for the annual shareholders' meeting. Instead, she was here, a glorified baby-sitter. She cursed the schedule that put the two techs on the same shift. She'd take it up with the deputy director at tomorrow's senior management meeting. For now, she was postponing her paperwork in order to make sure routine tasks went smoothly.

"Barge approaching," announced the new tech, Thuy Anh Larocque. "Normal docking pattern."

Heinz Javid, a tech with years of experience and a substance abuse problem, turned to his control panel and pressed a few keys. "External docking hatch depressurizing." Kapoor pretended to be absorbed by the data on the screen.

“Wait a minute.” Larocque sounded puzzled. "Ms. Kapoor, the barge is deviating from its docking approach pattern."

Kapoor rose and stood behind Larocque, looking over the younger woman's shoulder at the readouts. "Override its autopilot and bring it in," she ordered.

“Overriding," Larocque reported, punching keys. A moment later, she looked up helplessly. "No response from the barge's controls."

"What?" Kapoor looked at the console again.

"Helm control is unresponsive. Its heading is locked in."

Kapoor could see she was correct. Damned unusual for there to be two errors: first, that the auto navigator had been mis-programmed and then that someone had altered the override access codes and not informed them. Not bloody likely. Turning to Javid, she said, "Contact Simcoe Base. Find out if the new security chief changed helm control codes on us."

"Right," he replied, sounding unconcerned.

Larocque continued tapping her control keys. The expression on her face suddenly turned to one of horror. "The barge is on a collision course with Refinery Number Four!"

Kapoor waved her out of her seat and took over the controls. She found no errors in Larocque's computations. She quickly activated the station's comlink.

"Attention. This is Director of Operations Yumiko Kapoor speaking. We have a collision alert for Sectors Twelve through Nineteen, adjacent to Refinery Number Four. Evacuate immediately. I repeat, evacuate all sections adjacent to Refinery Number Four immediately."

As she repeated the message in Japanese, she imagined the panic as dock workers fled the endangered areas. She hoped they would all make it out in time.

With more interest in his voice than before, Javid said, "Major Eaglefeather reports no changes to the helm control codes, Ms. Kapoor"

"That must mean we have a security breach. Someone has gotten hold of our codes and locked us out."

"Collision is imminent." Larocque had taken over Javid's console. Kapoor noted her quick thinking. Experienced or not, that woman had a bright future with the Consortium, assuming she didn't perish here with the rest of them.

"Another few minutes," Larocque said.

*

From his cottage, Sixto Masika, surrounded by his comrades, listened to the intercepts. The static blocked whole passages, but they were not doing badly, considering that they were tapping into a secure channel between the Peacekeepers and the Consortium's mining stations.

"Consortium Control, this is Mining Station Two," a man's

voice broke through the static. "We have a barge out of control and heading straight for Refinery Number Four. See if you can divert its course with a repulser beam."

"Will a repulser beam have any effect?" demanded Magaly. She had begun pacing.

"No," Zaria said, her voice tense. "Not at that distance."

Magaly smiled.

The explosion lit up the night sky over most of Palmares' southern hemisphere. Palmaran officials received reports of sightings throughout the night.

In the outer office. Major Eaglefeather stood beside Captain Lobo, who sat hunched in front of a blank monitor. They had been there since Heinz Javid comlinked to ask if the barge's helm control codes had been altered. The major felt despair. He knew that the barge had collided with the station. The sensors had confirmed it. The only questions now were how many lives had been lost and how much damage had been done. Already the major was speculating. If it were sabotage, one thing was certain: there was a traitor among them.

"We've lost visual, Major." Captain Lobo didn't bother to hide his frustration as he tried to regain the signal.

Hoping that audio was still intact, the major shouted into the transmitter. "Yumiko Kapoor do you read me?"

Amid the static, a faint voice responded. "I read you, Major. The barge just collided with the refinery. That means we've lost over two thousand tons of quilidon. I must go. Our orbit is beginning to decay."

Colonel Welch stormed into the room. "I just heard. What's going on up there?"

Before the major could respond. Captain Lobo spoke up. "A

barge went out of control and crashed into one of the refineries."

"My God! Was it destroyed?"

He didn't ask about the dead, the major noticed.

"No report on that yet, sir," the captain replied smartly.

The major wondered whether the younger officer was trying to impress the colonel with his command of the situation, but he dismissed the thought as quickly as it had come. "The director of operations, Yumiko Kapoor, is trying to stabilize their orbit," he said. "We're waiting for word on their situation."

"What caused it?" the colonel demanded. "Human error? Sabotage?"

"The latter, I'd say," the major answered regretfully.

The colonel leaned toward the transmitter "Kapoor, this is Colonel Welch. I want a damage and casualty report and I want it now."

Kapoor's voice was barely audible over the static. " ... not available right now, Colonel. Our orbit has only just stabilized ... full report as information becomes available. Kapoor out."

o

Satisfied by the mission's success, a mission no one would ever link to them, Sixto and his comrades sat down to eat. As the domestic droid rolled in with lunch, they speculated about how much quilidon had been lost. Sixto was quiet throughout the meal. While the others were still eating, he pushed his half-full plate away. "Do you think there were any casualties?" he said.

Magaly could barely contain her irritation. "If there were it wasn't our fault. They had plenty of time to evacuate."

"We planned carefully to minimize the possibility of deaths or injuries, Sixto," Zaria said quietly.

"That's true, Sixto," Tariq agreed. "They had plenty of time to calculate the barge's course. Any idiot could have issued the order to evacuate the area."

"You pacifists!" Magaly threw her napkin on the table. "Do you think they worried themselves about Rabindra before they killed him? Do you think they shed a single tear over the people killed in the square?"

"Magaly," Sixto said evenly, "we must remain respectful of human life and remember our goal. If this turns into a killing contest, we'll lose. We don't have the technology to defeat them militarily."

"We did all right today," Magaly said. She stood abruptly and went into the kitchen.

Sixto sipped his tea. Tariq studied his plate, hands folded in his lap. Finally, Zaria rose. Sixto caught her hand. "She'll be all right."

Zaria pulled away. "I'm going to talk to her."

Magaly was standing by the nanowave, stirring mate in a cup. She looked up when Zaria entered. "He doesn't have what it takes to see this through, and you know it."

"Let's not talk about Sixto behind his back."

"If you really love him, Zaria, you'll face the truth. He's not up to it. And I don't really feel like listening to him whine about preserving Peacekeeper lives, not when I know what they've done to Rabindra and to Mayseung and Seth and others before them. And what they will do to countless others before our planet breaks up."

"He just has strong principles."

"And I don't?" She pushed the cup of mate away in disgust. "What do you think, Zaria? That we'll win this thing by civil disobedience? By demonstrations like the one in the square the other day? By caring more about their lives than our own?" She turned her back. "You've changed since you got involved with Sixto. You care more about pleasing him than you do about doing what has to

be done."

"That's not true! Well, maybe I have changed, a little, for the better. Sixto makes me think about things I wouldn't ordinarily think about. It doesn't do any harm to be reminded that war could cost us our humanity."

Magaly turned back to her. "Maybe not. So long as it doesn't stop you from doing what needs doing."

"It won't."

"Programmed by remote? How?" Colonel Welch leaned over Major Eaglefeather's console and watched the screen impatiently.

After being briefed in detail by Yumiko Kapoor, the major had prepared a report, but the colonel was too agitated to sit down and read it. He wanted immediate answers.

"By someone who had our helm codes," the major said. "They were also skilled navigators. Had to be."

The colonel glared at him. "I find it hard to believe that the Palmarans could pull this off on their own." For the colonel, Palmarans were simply inferior, incapable of planning and executing such an act. The major thought otherwise, but his intelligence reports told him that the Palmarans had neither the hardware nor the software such a complex operation would have required. No, it was much easier than that. Someone had handed over the codes. A sympathizer? A mercenary? He had no idea, but he shared the colonel's suspicions that the Palmarans could not have acted alone.

"We have a traitor in our midst," the colonel said, his irritation increasing as he talked. "A defector .Do you suppose that Sixto Masika fellow had some role in this?"

"I could only speculate at this point, Colonel."

"How will you proceed? Internal security alert? I suggest you have all personnel account for their ignition cards, forthwith." It was not really a suggestion, more like an order.

"I'll have Captain Lobo oversee all that, sir. But I don't think it will get us very far."

"Then what will?"

"I'm working on it, sir."

Chapter Nine

Cleaning droids were polishing the Aristide's tile floor when Major Eaglefeather walked in. Their noise echoed in the large vacant club. Never having seen the Aristide empty, he took a moment to look around. The club had no doors. Three patios allowed easy access, and while the open-concept design let the sea air circulate freely, it also conveyed a complete lack of concern about security. It surprised him that Nailah, a known collaborator, seemed unworried, but he supposed she might be taking some less-than-obvious precautions.

For the first time, he could see the reproductions of ancient musical instruments in the corners of the large room. Several small alcoves carved into the clay walls held holo-sculptures. Scenes from Palmaran history predominated.

One holo-sculpture — a still — had a coffee-skinned woman proudly holding a melon-like fruit. The caption underneath identified the woman only as Sarita, the first successful grower of cantamelon on Palmaran soil.

An active holo-sculpture depicted a drenching rainfall as seen from an orbiting spacecraft. Lightning crackled in the replicated sky. It was a recreation of the seeding that had converted the water vapour in the pre-terraformed Palmaran atmosphere to liquid. The rain had lasted for over three standard years, leaving the large oceans which now covered most of the planet's surface.

A third featured an old brown man standing on a red beach next to some machinery. The caption said that Avelino Machado had designed a system to accelerate the desalination of the seas.

He made his way to a fourth alcove. It held another active holo-sculpture, showing a group of young children of many colours, playing on an apparatus in an indoor activity centre. Although the children looked happy enough, the playroom was dim, colourless and overcrowded. The caption described the scene as typical of the children's play facilities aboard the Consortium ships that had brought the Palmaran's ancestors to work in the mines.

The major considered the collages of art, history and nationalism around him. If someone wanted to promote a cause, this was a quiet yet effective way to do it. Clearly, even Nailah saw Palmare's way of life threatened. That explained Palmaran hostility toward Terrans, but it did not excuse terrorism.

As he strode toward the stage, his boots clattering on the gleaming tile floor, he dodged Chihuahua-sized cleaning droids. About to conclude no one was in, he heard a rustling from backstage and Nailah appeared. Her delicate pastel parasilk robe billowed out behind her, emphasizing her graceful stride. At first he was surprised that he had interrupted her sleep at this time of day, but then he remembered that the Aristide stayed open until dawn and naturally Nailah and her troupe would not be early risers.

She glided towards him, looking puzzled. "Well, we haven't seen you for a while, Major. You're a bit early for the show."

"I'm not here to see the show." He was cordial yet firm. "I'm here to see Zaria."

"She's not here." He wondered what she thought about his trying to get to know her daughter. She seemed approving. More so than Zaria, in fact.

"Not here? After performing into the early morning hours, she's up and about?"

"I doubt it. She didn't perform last night. She went to Tubman to visit family. Probably got stuck there after curfew and couldn't get back to the compound. I can vidphone to see when she'll be back, if you like."

"No, you can't. Communications are offline. Colonel Welch's orders. He wants to make sure there's no unauthorized communication between Simcoe and other parts of the planet." There would be no more remote programming of the Consortium's barges. The major didn't say that he had vigorously opposed the order.

"Well, the downtime should prove just as inconvenient for you as for us."

"Probably." He had already dealt with some two dozen complaints that morning, most coming from Peacekeepers who had to put their duties and their personal dealings on hold to accommodate the communications black-out. Everything from food shipments to love affairs was being affected.

There was a light tapping on the wall behind him. He turned to see a haggard Major Stojic, standing in the shadow of a large tree in one of the Aristide's gardens. "Excuse me," Nailah said.

Stojic and Nailah exchanged some hushed words on the patio. He pressed something into her hands. Slipping the object discreetly into her flowing robes, Nailah walked back into the Aristide. "I'll just be a moment, Major," she assured Eaglefeather on her way backstage.

Stojic either did not see or ignored his colleague. It was odd behaviour for such a normally gregarious man, but Eaglefeather was relieved not to have to deal with him right now. Nailah returned moments later with a small package which she handed to Major Stojic. He left, without so much as a nod. He did not look well, the younger major observed.

"Tell me, is he an addict?" Eaglefeather asked frankly when Nailah returned to him.

Coveted because it was said to grant the user momentary telepathy, Bliss was strictly controlled and regulated by the Terran government. Although many doubted the drug's telepathic properties, the major knew that law enforcement officials on Basilea used it during criminal investigations and when interrogating suspects. No responsible person advocated its use as a recreational drug. Its addictive — and neuron-damaging —

properties were enough to ban its widespread use.

Nevertheless, many claimed that the restrictions on Bliss were politically motivated, that the evidence of its adverse effects was fabricated. Telepathy in the hands of "the wrong people," after all, would threaten the ruling classes everywhere. Those who illicitly used Bliss claimed to be engaging in acts of protest. Despite the arguments, the major thought that consuming Bliss was an act of stupidity, given the health risks involved.

"I don't know," she answered shortly.

"And don't care? So long as you get paid?"

She was unperturbed. "This is not Earth, Major Eaglefeather. Bliss is legal here and not very expensive. I am hardly getting rich."

"It's not legal within the compound," he argued, although he was well aware that official policy ignored its use, so as not to further antagonize the Palmaran government. It was a policy with which he felt uneasy. True, he had no interest in further damaging relations with the Palmarans, yet the freedom with which Bliss was bought and sold in the compound made smuggling both easy and lucrative.

"The Consortium doesn't make the law here," Nailah informed him. "The Palmaran Governing Council does."

"If you could see what that stuff does to kids on Earth, you'd know why it's illegal there."

Nailah remained unrepentant. "Whatever is wrong with your youth, you cannot blame Bliss. Many Palmarans use it. Some to relax, some for medicinal purposes, some for spiritual reasons. But no one is addicted."

"I find that hard to believe."

"Perhaps you should ask yourself why your young people want to escape into drugs in the first place. And then you should probably decriminalize it, so it's not so lucrative that dealers will kill each other and innocent bystanders for the right to sell it."

"Oh that sounds like a perfect idea. Maybe we should make it available in candy stores. Or better yet, add it to infant formula."

"That ale you drink probably does your body more harm than

Bliss, Major Eaglefeather"

"You Palmarans are so self-righteous."

"That may be true," she smiled, "but we know how to have a good time."

He winced. "My god! If you only knew who else said that..."

"I know who else says it, Major. And if there is anything to admire about Major Stojic, it's his honesty. I'd rather deal directly with bigotry."

"Have I just been insulted?" he asked incredulously.

Nailah sighed heavily. "Have you had breakfast yet, Major?"

"Breakfast?"

"Yes, breakfast. Major The morning meal? Why don't we sit and have some? I'm hungry."

He hesitated.

"I promise not to lace it with Bliss." She looked amused as she led him to a table. "Lorangs for two," she said to the headwaiter.

"Lorangs?" Eaglefeather had never heard of them.

"It's a mildly sweet fruit," she said. "Locally grown."

He nodded. "As long as we're on the topic of local consumption habits, do you mind if I ask another sensitive question?"

"Anything to help promote cross-cultural awareness."

"Are Palmarans vegetarians for religious reasons?"

Her grey dreadlocks bounced as she threw her head back in a hearty laugh. "I see you've taken Major Stojic's anthropology course." He blushed. "For some, there are religious reasons. And, of course, there are many other reasons, like good health and animal rights. But the main reason is economic."

"Non-meat foods are cheaper?"

"We are land-poor" she explained, "and it takes more land to raise animals than it does to grow food for people. It doesn't make sense to turn over what little land we have to cows or goats. We can feed more people with an acre of maize than we can with the meat from an acre of grazing land."

"That makes sense."

"Yes. Surprising, isn't it?"

The droid arrived with their food. Eaglefeather liked the lorangs. Their thick skins had been peeled back, and their pits removed. They were about the size of tangerines.

"There is a great deal of misunderstanding between our two people," he remarked, between bites. "It makes the prospect of peace seem very unlikely."

Before Nailah could respond, Zaria came in from one of the patios, flanked by Tariq and a lovely woman he had previously seen in his company. That would be Persis, he thought, remembering his intelligence reports. Zaria smiled. He wondered how long that would last, given his reason for being here.

"Major," she called out, "you're becoming my biggest fan."

"I need to talk to you."

She frowned. "Good morning to you too. Or should I salute?"

"Take it easy on the young major, Zaria," Nailah said. "Having breakfast with me has left him a little unsettled."

"May we talk? Please?" There was an awkward pause as the major realized that he was being rude, but he had an important reason for being here, and he needed to get on with it.

"Of course," Zaria replied, after a nod from her mother "Why don't we walk along the beach?"

Chapter Ten

Zaria led the major down the cliff to the beach, where they could talk privately. They walked along the shoreline, barefooted, swinging their shoes in their hands, quiet at first. He was finding it difficult to broach the subject he had come to discuss. Zaria hoped it wasn't personal and braced herself for a declaration of love. She waited tensely, unable to enjoy the sun's warmth on her face and the salt wind in her hair.

"This reminds me of back home," he finally said. "The sun, the sea air, the beach. The colours are different and the smell, of course. Nothing smells quite like a Terran beach."

"You mean that dead fish and seaweed smell?"

"That's the one," he laughed. "It's been a while since I've had the pleasure of walking on a beach. Most of the water on Basilea is permafrost.

"It is lovely here, isn't it?" she said. "And the Consortium has managed to lay claim to the most beautiful spot on the planet."

"Didn't your people sign a treaty that gives the Consortium the right to be here? For two hundred years?"

"It was the only way we could win home rule. Unfortunately, our grandparents had a rather limited understanding of the concept. Or maybe they had no choice about signing the deal. But what good is home rule? We aren't independent and we don't control our resources."

"It was an important treaty, the first of its kind. It became a model for other colonies."

"I'm sure it did," she shot back. "Colonizers throughout history have recognized the cost-effectiveness of indirect control. Give people the right to elect their own leaders, fund their own security forces, health care and education, but maintain control of their resources and you can still call the tune. It's an old strategy — once called neo-colonialism by dissidents on Earth. Political independence alone means little."

"I'm surprised to hear you complaining. You benefit from the arrangement. Off-worlders, Consortium employees. Peacekeepers — they all spend money at the Aristide."

She caught her reply in her throat, then said, "So I gather you've been a busy security chief lately. The comcasts say the barge accident was sabotage."

The major went easily with the change of subject. "Sabotage is no accident. And yes, I've been busy."

She stopped walking and faced him, her hands on her hips and her eyes angry. "So are you here to interrogate me? Am I a suspect?"

"I ran a routine security check on your family. Why didn't you tell me that you'd been to Earth? That your father was a Peacekeeper? That you were trained as a Peacekeeper pilot?"

For a moment she said nothing. "Why would you check up on me and my family?" she said indignantly.

"It's my job. I have to eliminate suspects."

"So am I a suspect?"

"Technically, yes," he admitted. "But there are more likely candidates around."

"Why would I be a suspect?"

"The Aristide is one of the few places on this planet where Palmarans, Consortium employees and Peacekeepers fraternize freely. It's the perfect cover for an intelligence-gathering operation."

"You must be kidding. If you only knew what my mother has gone through because she serves the Terran community. Other Palmarans hate us. Besides, if I'm a spy, I must be a very bad one."

"Why do you say that?"

"Because we haven't been to bed yet." She was pleased with the blush he gave her in response. "Surely you must have better suspects."

"I do. Too many to narrow down. That's why I'm here. I'd like you to help me."

She resumed her stroll, and he kept pace with her. "Why should I help you?" she asked. "Better yet, why should you trust me?"

"Because I think you want peace. Because you don't hate Terrans. Because I don't believe you're a spy. You speak your mind too freely."

Zaria bit back a smile. The very behaviour that ought to have frustrated her attempts to get close to the major was winning his confidence.

"Will you help me?"

She cautioned herself not to accept too readily. "How will helping you capture your saboteur bring peace to Palmares?"

"It will be an example of how a Palmaran and a Terran can cooperate."

She considered it. "The Kituhwa would kill me."

"We have to learn to get along. It has to start somewhere. If the terrorists can be put down, Terran resources can be invested into stabilizing this planet, rather than spent on security."

"So I should do it for my planet?"

"I know how you feel. I'm going after one of my own people on this too. A traitor, a defector."

"Are you sure there is one?" Terrans could not credit Palmarans with even the slightest ingenuity, she fumed to herself.

"No offense, but Palmarans could not have programmed that barge without Terran help. They'd have had to have the access codes."

True. We had access codes. But we have no Terran allies, "So working together, we bring a Palmaran and a Terran to justice and peace will reign. Is that the idea?" She fought to keep her tone light.

"It's a first step. Somebody has to take it."

"What would you want me to do?"

"You say you used to live in Tubman."

"Yes. Our family house is still there."

"Sixto Masika lives there, too, I understand."

"Yes. That's no secret. You suspect he's your saboteur?"

He frowned. "I suspect — strongly suspect — that he's involved with the Kituhwa."

"You and everyone else on the planet, but no one's found any proof."

"I'm close. Think back a few weeks — don't you remember the comcasts that we'd caught a Kituhwa saboteur in the act? A Rabindra Woczek. Only nineteen years old."

Zaria made herself look at the major. She wasn't sure she was up to hearing him tell her his part in Rabindra's death. "Right. I remember. He was killed, wasn't he?"

The major kept his voice level. "Yes. It was unfortunate — an accident."

He sounded uneasy with Rabindra's death. He might regret it, she supposed, but she didn't ask for details. She didn't want to know and she had to keep in character. "And you think he was connected to Masika?"

"He was a student of Masika's, enrolled in his first year geology course. He was also a karate student at a dojo owned and operated by a Magaly Uxmal. Ever heard of her?"

"No," Zaria lied.

"We've identified her as one of Masika's bodyguards."

"Tenuous connection, at best, isn't it? I mean, there must be dozens, even hundreds, of people studying both. What's it prove?" She forced herself to stop talking.

"Perhaps. But it's likely that Masika Uxmal and the young man were more than teachers and students. But I need your help if I'm to get proof."

"What would you want me to do?"

"Tubman is a small quilombo. You must know him."

"I know him quite well." It wasn't a lie. She did know him quite well, she said to herself.

"Then you can get close to him, physically close? I mean maybe get into his house?"

This time she had to smile. "I think so."

"Good. If Masika isn't the saboteur himself, I think he can probably lead me to him or her. But I need your help."

Sixto Masika fingered the wafer-thin white device. He turned it over and over in his hand as Magaly and Zaria looked on. Magaly was growing impatient. She didn't like to be reminded of the technology gap between the Palmarans and the Terrans.

"How do you turn it on?" Sixto asked Zaria for the second time. She whipped out the hand-held remote control. "I activate and deactivate by remote, by pressing here ..." She pointed to the button.

For the second time she went over the major's instructions. She was to plant the imager in Sixto's cottage, the ceiling would be best, if she could manage it. That way, the major would get a wide-angle view of what went on in the cottage. The casing would change colour to blend in with its surroundings, making it unnoticeable.

"This should come in handy," Sixto said, handing the imager to Magaly. "Have Tariq take it apart. If we learn how it works, we can build more."

Magaly's patience had come to an end. "That sounds fine. But what about Major Eaglefeather? He suspects us. He's not going to leave us alone. What do we do about him?"

"I agree," Sixto said. "He is dangerous. Do you think he suspects you, Zaria? Maybe all this is a ploy, a trap." Magaly nodded, satisfied that he was finally taking the threat seriously.

"I don't know," Zaria said. "My mother set up an incident to help me gain his trust. He seems sincere. He believes there's a traitor helping us. He sounds like he's as intent on catching the traitor as he is on catching the saboteur"

"There is no traitor," Magaly said. "Just some loose-lipped Peacekeepers."

"But as long as the major thinks I can lead him to his traitor" said Sixto, "as long as he uses Zaria to find the saboteur, everyone at the Aristide is in great danger. If the major really trusts Zaria to help him, he's going to expect her to deliver. And when she doesn't... He might suspect you already, Zaria, and this could be a set-up to get to the rest of us."

"Fine," Magaly said, pleased that Sixto had just made her case. "We have no choice. We have to kill him. And we can bring him here with his own device."

"No." Sixto stared at Magaly.

"I'm not convinced that it's necessary," said Zaria, playing for time. "There must be other ways. Let's think about it, Magaly."

Magaly inhaled sharply. "I have thought about it. What does it take to convince you? When they come for you? When they kill Sixto? Look, Zaria, if he's told you that much, then he's already investigating the dojo and Sixto's classes. Just how long do you think he's going to need to connect Mayseung and Seth, captured last year, to my dojo? To Sixto's classes? How long before he finds out that you and I went to school together?"

She was right, and Zaria knew it. They could all end up like Rabindra. Sixto, Magaly, Nailah — all of them. Her need for Sixto's approval was clouding her judgement. Magaly had warned her. Feeling her throat constrict, Zaria said, "She's right, Sixto. There are too many lives at stake. We can't take the risk." Magaly smiled in triumph.

"But there are other ways, Zaria. Surely you can see that?" Sixto countered.

"Like what?" Magaly pressed. "We can't shut down the Aristide. It's our only intelligence-gathering operation inside the compound."

"I don't know whether that will be necessary," countered Sixto, "but I'll shut down the operation at the Aristide before I'll agree to killing anybody."

"Really?" sneered Magaly. "Well, you appear to be in the

minority."

"Zaria," Sixto asked, "is that what you want? To assassinate the major?"

She studied the remote control. "I don't see any other way, Sixto. We've gone through the logic. Now that he's connected Rabindra to the dojo ..."

Sixto set his jaw. "If you two are going to make plans to take a human life, you can do it somewhere else. And count me out."

"Fine with me," Magaly said. She grabbed her knapsack and walked out.

Unable to think of anything worth saying, Zaria slowly slipped on her jacket and left. Magaly was waiting for her outside, but Zaria was in no mood to hear her rant about Sixto's pacifism. She frowned as Magaly fell into step beside her. After a few minutes, the small woman said, "Thanks for backing me up, Zaria. I know it wasn't easy for you."

"I didn't do it for you. I did it because I don't see any other way."

At this, her friend nodded. "Nevertheless, I'm sure it was difficult. I'm sorry."

"Thanks," Zaria muttered.

After a pause, Magaly continued. "You're one of the few people who realize I don't enjoy all of this." When Zaria said nothing she added, "You do realize that, don't you?"

"Of course I do." Zaria emphasized this with a squeeze of her friend's shoulder.

"Now here's what I've got in mind ..."

Chapter Eleven

The major was having difficulty concentrating on the data on his screen. He hadn't seen Zaria in a week, though he knew she had returned from Tubman. In her absence, he had worried about her safety, debated with himself about whether he'd been right to ask for her help. If the Kituhwa found out what she was doing, they would kill her.

They could barely speak to each other without getting into a political debate, yet he welcomed those debates, enjoyed them, thought about them afterward. He admired her, and not just for speaking her mind. She was headstrong, yes, but she made sense a lot of the time. The more he could see Palmares through her eyes, the better he would understand her people, and that could only help him. And maybe it would put him in a position to help bring peace to this world.

Catching sight of Captain Lobo coming into the outer office, the major began to tap at the keys. The captain had been assigned to monitor the transmissions that had begun yesterday from Sixto Masika's house in Tubman quilombo. Nothing of interest had transpired in the first twenty recorded hours. Now, the briskness of his walk made the major ask him if he had something.

"We just received this a few minutes ago, sir. I'll play it back." Captain Lobo placed a cube into the holo-imager atop the major's console and depressed a button. An image from within Masika's cottage took shape.

A miniature Sixto Masika sat pecking at a computer keyboard.

He appeared to be putting together a grocery order. Music laced with heavy percussion played in the background. Seen from the ceiling, the cottage looked modest, clean, and neat. The floor was tiled in a simple geometric pattern. The walls were of white clay. A domestic droid rolled across the scene, busy at some household chore. Masika was dressed casually, but his gleaming copper dreadlocks testified to the care he gave them. A buzzer rang. His fingers halted over the keyboard. Pressing a button, he checked his screen. Apparently satisfied with what he saw, he pressed another button to release the door.

A small woman the major had by now identified as Magaly Uxmal entered. Her name was almost all he knew about her. Once a card-carrying Menchista, she had disappeared at the time of the Kituhwa split. No information had been gathered on her since then. No one had considered her important enough.

Masika spun his chair around to face her. "Sorry to bother you," Uxmal told him. "I just met with our contact. There seems to be some trouble. A meeting for tonight has been requested. Here."

"Why?" he demanded, rising. "What kind of trouble?"

She gestured her ignorance. "I don't know. Additional security measures. He thought we would want to know about them."

"And so we would," he assured her. "Tonight sounds fine. Make it midnight. But not here. At the Merae Goree. Confirm it."

"Yes, sir," Uxmal pronounced crisply, and left.

With a smile, the captain switched off the imager. "We've got him, sir. How about I round up some troops and head out to Merae Goree, wherever that is?"

The major didn't answer immediately. There was still no evidence that Sixto Masika had been involved in sabotaging the barge, and the contact they spoke of could have been anyone. Besides, Peacekeepers did not have jurisdiction outside Simcoe, a fact he reminded the captain of.

"Are you telling me we can't touch Masika? He gets away with it? Is that what you're saying?"

"Hold on." The major raised his hands to underscore the point. "We have no evidence that he was involved at all. One thing at a time. If we find the traitor we might find a link."

"And what if we get something on Masika? Extradition? That could take years!" As the captain objected, the major turned to his console and tapped in a sequence of codes. "The station has no reference to a location called Merae Goree."

"I think we should probably check all databases, sir. It could be a code name."

The major had already initiated the search. "Here's something," he announced. "Merae. A Maori word. A community gathering space in a Maori kainga or village."

"The Kituhwa do that all the time," said the captain impatiently. "They take words from dead languages and make code words out of them. Isn t there another reference?"

"No," the major replied absently. "Interesting. Goree Island is off the coast of Senegal, West Africa, on Earth. It was a holding centre for African slaves several centuries ago. It's some sort of monument now. Tourist attraction."

"Very interesting, sir. But where does that get us?'

They called up map after map of the local terrain, but an hour later had yet to find Merae Goree. "It's a code name. So now what. Major?"

Rising, the major said, "I think I can find out. I have some local contacts who might know."

"I wouldn't trust any of the informants we've used in the past, sir. They're all afraid of the Kituhwa. They just might fatally mislead you. It's happened before."

"It's no one we've used in the past," the major said vaguely.

"Oh?" The captain's tone made his resentment at not being taken into the major's confidence obvious. "Who then?"

"I'd rather keep my contacts to myself, Captain. I prefer to build a personal relationship with informants. Develops trust."

"I see. And what if this contact tells you the location of Merae Goree?"

"I'll proceed tonight."

"Good," the captain said, satisfied. "I'll have a contingent on standby."

"I can't go out there with troops. That would be a violation of the treaty we have with the Palmaran government."

Captain Lobo did not care about that, but he did care about antagonizing his commanding officer so he chose not to pursue the matter. "In that case, will you take a homing device, sir?"

"All right, Captain."

"And what are your orders if we lose contact?"

"Give me four hours before you take any action." The captain would have to satisfy himself with monitoring the homing signal and keeping a rescue team at the ready. The major signed out the equipment he would need, then headed for the Aristide.

It was night, but not very dark. The club brimmed with patrons, eating and dancing. Few tried to talk above the holo-band. The major searched the crowd for Zaria. He found her, in costume, talking to Tariq and Persis. When their eyes met, he waved for her to join him and chose a vacant table in the rear

"Is your device proving useful?" she asked, her grass skirt rustling as she sat down across from him. A trace of sweat glistened between her breasts, a sign that she had already performed tonight. He was sorry he'd missed it.

"Very," he said. "I need to know about a place called Merae Goree."

"Not much to know. Merae is the name given to places of ritual and celebration. Every quilombo has its own. Tubman's is called Merae Goree. I doubt you could find it on your own. But I could take you there."

He took a moment to consider the offer. It might be dangerous for her. Then again, he wasn't about to get involved in a confrontation. He would find out what he could, get evidence, if possible, and it would probably save time to have her along as a guide. He would also enjoy her company. "I'd appreciate your help," he told her. "But we'd better leave now. Masika is meeting someone there at midnight and I want to see who."

"Your traitor?" He nodded. Zaria leaned back, her arms across her chest. "We have to go alone, Major. I won't lead trigger-happy troops into a quilombo full of elders and children."

He nodded again. "I understand."

"Are you armed?" Unsure of how she would react, he avoided answering. "Never mind. You probably have a signalling device. Your friends will find you wherever you go." He grinned in return. "You're welcome to search me if you like."

One eyebrow shot up. "As delightful as that sounds, Major, I'd be wasting my time — any transmitter would be subcutaneous." His smile widened. He had forgotten that she had trained as a Peacekeeper. She knew about the implant and she knew he was armed. "I don't know how to make you trust me, Zaria. If it makes you feel any better, I'm taking a risk trusting you."

"Then why did you ask for my help?" He was not sure himself. He was afraid that his main reason might have been to set up a situation that would require them to spend time together, get to know each other. That she proved so helpful was luck. "Because I needed it. Are we going or not?"

"Can you get us a skip? Without military markings?"

"A stratoskip? I've already signed one out. It's in the ground lot."

"Wait here. I'll change." She rose and left. He watched her skirt swish as she walked backstage.

"What did the headwaiter read?" Zaria asked her brother. Tariq looked up from the console. "Well, he's got an erection."

"Tariq!" Zaria was not amused. She hated this. Being the object of Sixto's contempt was painful enough. He hadn't spoken to her since the night she had decided to help draw the major to Tubman. She and Magaly had faked the hologram without his cooperation, and it hadn't been easy, but they'd done it, and the major had fallen for it. He was probably falling in love with her. She shuddered. None of this felt right. But the mission had progressed too far now. There was no going back.

"He's transmitting a constant signal," Tariq reported, studying the readings. "From his right forearm. Probably a homing device. Standard-issue handweapon in his left chest area, no surprise. No special equipment of any kind that I can pick up."

Zaria nodded in acknowledgment. "Contact Magaly. Tell her I'm on my way." With that, she left to change.

The major was studying the control readouts much more intently than was necessary. Zaria wondered if he felt uneasy being alone with her. She could have relieved him of the burden of striking up a conversation, but she lacked the energy and her conscience balked at continuing to cultivate a friendship that would end in betrayal.

She turned her attention to the familiar stratoskip console in front of her. The opportunity to fly came so infrequently these days. She had trained on a skip not unlike this one. She had enjoyed flying. It was one of the few things about her Peacekeeping training that she had enjoyed. She looked around her. The skip had seating room for four, with minimal storage space. Fixed to the back of the major's seat was a standard-issue Peacekeeper's kit. She could only guess what might be inside, and her guesses worried her. She considered scanning it with the skip's internal equipment — she did not want any unpleasant surprises for Magaly — but there was no way she could gain access to the skip's controls without the major noticing.

Taking the direct approach, she asked, "What's in the kit?"

"Holo-imager," he said. "Sound equipment. To gather evidence. I'm hoping we can find a spot where we can observe the meeting without being seen. Can we do that?"

"I suppose." She hoped he was telling the truth. "You should switch to silent mode now."

Silent mode was not really silent, but the low hum the stratoskip emitted could not be heard over the waves and the wind on the cliff side of Merae Goree. While power remained diverted to the engine's muting mechanism, the stratoskip's speed would be cut in half, and its weapons system would be offline.

They looked down on green plots speckling the copper landscape. A terraforming droid was crawling up a slight incline. Zaria told the major that there were several hundred droids roaming the planet on year-long missions, working the soil and seeding it with foodstuffs. Despite the droids' ability to work day and night, the task was painfully slow.

They skirted the shoreline. In the middle of the dark purple sea, they flew over a patch of deep green. "What was that?" the major asked.

"Hydroponic farm. Experimental. But, as you can see, they are getting some things to grow."

"Incredible. This is a beautiful planet."

The rolling red hills looked eerie against the dim violet sky. Ahead of them, a moon was just rising over the horizon and would soon fill a large part of the sky. "Yes, it is beautiful," she said.

"No, I mean it," he insisted. "It's one of the most beautiful places I've ever seen. And I don't look at beauty superficially. I take it all in — the landscape, the people, the history, the culture — all of it. It's beautiful." He turned to her suddenly and smiled. Under other circumstances, she would have smiled back, but she could not. Instead, she bit her lip and turned away.

They made the approach to Merae Goree, a plateau atop a spectacular cliff. Clay poles held up a thatched roof. There were no walls. The major would find out later that the spot was comfortably shaded, with a fresh breeze from the sea. A sparse, well-trampled lawn lay just in front of a modest structure and a lush, thick garden spread past Merae Goree to cover most of the plateau. It was a spot to rival the finest of English gardens, a haven in the harsh, barren terrain. Zaria could almost smell the flowers. She pointed to her left. "That's Goree." He nodded in appreciation. "Better cut your lights."

"Is there anywhere to set down, besides that clearing?" He made a note of the time on his chronometer. She was tempted to tell him not to worry about the time. Magaly would wait.

"There's an outcropping below the edge of the cliff. There."

He looked and shook his head. "It's too small. I can't land there."

His reluctance did not surprise Zaria. She had made the landing many times, her fear diminishing only gradually. "Sure you can. There's room to spare."

"No," he said. "The wind is too strong out here. We'll smash into the side of the cliff. I'll find somewhere else."

"I can do it. Transfer the controls to me." He hesitated. "Don't worry. I'm a trained pilot, remember?" As the console lit up before her, she congratulated herself.

On touchdown, the major sighed more heavily than Zaria thought fair. "Nice job," he muttered, unclenching his hands from the armrests.

They climbed out of the stratoskip quickly. The major walked to the edge of the cliff and cautiously leaned forward to look at the rocky beach some fifty metres below. The rocks had fallen from the cliff; some had once been only centimetres from where he stood. Below, waves wore away at the side of the cliff.

Zaria stayed by the skip, watching him. He returned from his walkabout and looked up the cliff at the plateau twenty-five or so metres above them. "Now, how do we get up there?"

"There are some steps carved into the rock over there." She pointed to a place hidden in the cliff's face. The incline above was not as sheer as the drop below them, but it would be like climbing a ladder most of the way.

The major ducked into the stratoskip and opened the kit. Zaria peered over his shoulder. She saw him unpack a holo-imager but did not recognize the rest of the equipment. He also pulled out a five-centimetre-long cylinder, which she surmised was some sort of recording device. He packed the equipment into a sturdy backpack, which he then slipped on. Adjusting its weight, he said, "Let's go."

With Zaria leading, they climbed. The stone steps zigzagged sharply, to avoid the steeper areas. She could hear his laboured breathing behind her reminding her that he was still adjusting to the planet's atmosphere. "We'll be in thick brush when we reach the top," she said. "I think we should stay under its cover until we know what's going on."

"Let's see when we get there." He would take no more advice from her now, she thought, but it really didn't matter much at this point.

She reached the top and turned to watch him heave himself up to join her. The change in the landscape was startling, even for Zaria, who had made the climb many times. They found themselves in the rainforest. Foliage blocked the reflected moonlight and they could see only vague shapes. Sweet garden smells permeated the darkness. A narrow path, cushioned with decaying vegetation, stretched out before them.

The major paused and looked around. She knew he would also be listening for movements, even sniffing the air for what it might tell him about what or who was nearby. She waited patiently until he was satisfied. He put a finger to his lips and waved her closer. She should, he said, remain there and wait for him. If anything went wrong, she was to climb down to the stratoskip and get help. She nodded compliantly. It made no difference now.

Cautiously, he stepped onto the path. He had walked only a few metres when the dense growth behind him rustled. By the time he turned around Huseni and Rahim were on him, Huseni's boot striking the back of his knee. Rahim hit from the front, and once the major's momentum had brought him to the ground, Rahim had his arms. Zaria ducked as the major's handweapon, already in his grasp, discharged and scorched a tree beside her. Rahim had the major's right arm locked in a hold that threatened to dislocate his shoulder.

With the major firmly pinned to the ground, Magaly walked out of darkness. She held her weapon steady and pointed it at the major.

Zaria rushed forward to seize his weapon. He immediately stopped struggling. "I should have known," was all he said.

Chapter Twelve

As they were climbing the cliff, the major had begun to question the wisdom of allowing Zaria to accompany him. To protect her, he had asked her to wait behind. As his knees gave way under the first attacker's boot, he had unholstered his weapon. If he could keep the attackers busy she could make her escape. As he fought, he saw Magaly Uxmal come towards him, looking from his vantage point on the ground not that much larger than her hologram image. Then he saw a shadow behind him.

It seemed to him as if Zaria was acting in slow motion as she wrested his weapon away. Anger welled up inside him. The revelation of her treachery struck him with a force much greater than the two men holding him down could ever muster.

I should have known, he thought, watching her as she stepped over him to stand beside Magaly. Then he realized he had said it aloud.

"He's alone," Zaria coldly told Magaly. "There's a transmitter, a homing device, implanted in his right forearm."

The men who had him pinned released their grip. The major was unlikely to cause trouble with Magaly pointing an antique laser weapon at his midsection. As the major pulled himself to his knees, two more figures stepped out of the darkness. Sixto Masika and Almond Eyes.

Zaria started. "Sixto! Keoki! What are you doing here?"

Calmly, Masika positioned himself beside Zaria. Taking the major's weapon from her hand, he said, "he came alone, with only a handweapon. You two should be embarrassed. All your careful precautions for this?"

She said nothing. It seemed to the major that Masika's presence disturbed her.

Magaly turned to one of the men. "Kill him and throw the body off the cliff."

Alarm registered on Masika's face. He looked at Zaria. "Can you really do this?" The other two men exchanged uncertain glances.

"Sixto, don't interfere," said Magaly. "You're the visionary. My job is security. Now, go home!" To her comrades she shouted, "Do it!" The major braced himself for the discharge.

"No!" an emphatic voice commanded.

"I don't believe this!" Magaly's face reddened and her neck muscles grew taut. "Zaria, what are you doing? He came here to kill us. If not all of us, at least the man you claim to love. You want me to turn him loose to try again?"

The major felt like he'd been slapped. Masika was Zaria's lover. What a fool he had been. He'd been set up from the beginning, manipulated and manoeuvred like a kid.

"We should question him," Masika persisted. "He might be useful. He knows a lot about the Peacekeepers' activities."

"He's also a trained killer," Magaly countered.

"I didn't come here to kill you."

"No, just to gather evidence against us," Magaly responded. Zaria must have told her that, the major realized.

"Enough," Zaria bellowed, her anger matching Magaly's. "Sixto is right. We should question him first. He may have important information."

Shaking her head in disbelief, Magaly glared at Zaria. "You're making a big mistake."

"Take him down to the quilombo," Zaria ordered the men, who nodded obediently.

"They're going to come looking for him," Magaly objected.

Masika waved his hand in dismissal. "We have an alibi." He exchanged glances with Keoki, who smiled, checked his chrono and nodded. "Major, that little eavesdropping imager of yours has just been rendered useless in a scene performed to convince your friends that we found the device and destroyed it." To Magaly he said, "You're not the only one who can fake a hologram." He turned back to Eaglefeather. "We sounded typically paranoid, I assure you, Major"

"Let's go," Zaria urged.

"Peacekeepers will be all over this place by morning if I don't get back to the base," the major argued. He sounded desperate. With effort, he softened his tone. "I'd hate to see your village endangered. You should let me go."

Zaria took a step toward him. "They won't bother us once they find the burned-out wreckage of the skip at the bottom of the cliff. It will look like you tried to land on the ledge and crashed. The explosion and fire will destroy any trace of evidence. They will assume your body is lost at sea."

No wonder she had insisted on landing on the ledge. It would be that much easier to catapult the skip off the cliff. Whatever else she was, Zaria was no fool.

"There's one more thing," Magaly said abruptly. She walked up to the major signalling to her colleagues. "Hold his arm." The two men obeyed, one holding the major's right arm and the other restraining the rest of his body.

Magaly's weapon went off, the beam barely visible. The major winced in pain as it cut into his flesh. He stiffened and the men holding him tightened their grip. Magaly cut deeper than necessary. Then her fingers reached into his wound to pull out the transmitter. The major cried out as blood poured down his arm. When the three men released him, he was trembling in shock and pain.

"Did you have to do that?" Masika's voice shook in anger

Zaria grabbed her lover's arm. There was a look of revulsion on her face, but it was she who said, "I'm afraid so. The homing device must be destroyed."

Through his agony, Eaglefeather managed to snarl, "Gee, I'm sorry about all this bleeding. I hope it isn't making you uncomfortable."

Zaria let go of Masika's arm and pulled a handkerchief from her pocket. The major lay motionless as she wrapped it around his arm. It was white, trimmed with lace, he noticed, but even before she tied it off, it had turned crimson.

Magaly, after a brief examination of the pea-sized transmitter, dropped it to the dirt and ground it to pieces with the heel of her boot. She said, without any apparent emotion, "Better stop the bleeding before you move him. You don't want to leave a trail."

"Keoki and Huseni, go with Magaly and take care of the skip," Zaria barked. "Rahim, you're with us. Let's go, Major." She pulled him to his feet, exhibiting more strength than he would have anticipated.

Whether it was Masika or Zaria who called the shots was unclear. But at least Magaly was not in control. He would have to figure out which had the most influence. His life might depend on knowing that. At least that was what his training was telling him. But he hoped he would not have to humiliate himself before Zaria. Once on his feet, he swayed dizzily. Hands grabbed at him, steadied him, then began to half-carry, half-drag him.

As they climbed the cliff toward the quilombo, Zaria no longer doubted that what she had done was wrong. She had humiliated the major, but it was done, and there was no way to undo it. At least she hadn't killed him. Not yet, anyway. She was grateful for that on two counts: she liked the major and did not want to see him die, and keeping him alive might get her back in Sixto's good graces.

She hoped Sixto knew what he was doing. She sneaked a glance at the major, still conscious but bobbing listlessly between Sixto and Rahim, who were supporting most of his weight. What are we going to do with him? If he made it back to the base, he'd have them all arrested: Nailah, Tariq, Persis and the rest. Sixto would surely be killed. They couldn't let him go. Not now, not ever.

They would have to keep him prisoner. They had never taken prisoners. It seemed almost as wrong as killing him, but at least he would live. How long would they have to hold him? They had no facilities for him. Where would they keep him?Who would guard him twenty-eight hours a day? If he had told anyone about his plans for this evening, the quilombo would be crawling with Peacekeepers by dawn.

"You all right?" Rahim called to her from behind. Zaria had stopped and was blocking the path.

"Yes," she called back, and began climbing again.

Chapter Thirteen

The major felt himself being half-carried down the hill by Masika and a man with an earring. His arm was throbbing and, though he could hear conversation, following its thread proved too much for him. All he could gather was that they were satisfied with what they had accomplished.

He had no sense of how far they had brought him, but he figured they'd been on the move for less than an hour when they reached a group of low pink and red clay structures, typically Palmaran. A few lights shone through windows, in spite of the late hour. The group had followed a red-tiled path that wound through the gardens, plazas and homes of the quilombo till it reached an immense translumium greenhouse, filled with harvested crops resting in row after row of waist-high beds. His captors had expertly negotiated the long aisles and corners and he had lost track of the many turns they had taken. In the distance, he could hear waves lapping at the shore. It was quiet and they seemed to be alone.

Finally, they left the massive greenhouse, and Zaria led them to a door in a high, white-washed wall. Through it, they entered the ornate front garden of a two-story building. A balcony overlooked a small courtyard. Bright curtains hung in the large windows of what was clearly a private home. An unlikely prison, he thought. Zaria, still in the lead, opened the unlocked door. "Bring him in," she ordered her comrades.

"Are you sure this is a good idea?" Masika asked,

redistributing the major's weight. Zaria was already inside. Masika and Rahim followed, the major supported between them. "I'm not known to the Peacekeepers," she said. "You are. If anything goes wrong, where do you think they'll look first? Put him over there." Sixto and Rahim lowered him into a reclining chair. Someone turned on the lights. The major eased himself back and studied the room.

The clay walls were a tranquil green, with hologrammed family portraits on display in several alcoves. There was an abundance of plants, a computer console, two pallets covered in bright prints and a beautiful carpet warming the tiled floor. A batiked print, the major guessed it might be of West African design, hung on one wall. The shelf underneath it held clay pots, straw mats, wood and soapstone carvings, and a calabash. Beneath the shelf sat an array of percussion instruments, including drums of many sizes. A dreamcatcher hanging in a corner of the room caught his eye. Its familiar shape brought him comfort, the hope that he might have something in common with his captors after all.

The holograms portrayed Nailah, Tariq, Persis and others. There were portraits of Zaria as a baby, as a child and as a young woman. Bitterness flooded the major as he saw her face reproduced over and over.

From an adjoining room, he heard clattering and the sound of running water. Thin Nose — Huseni, Zaria had called him — and Magaly stood under the dreamcatcher, whispering to each other. From a third room, he heard an unfamiliar whirring sound, growing louder. It was not a domestic droid.

Magaly and Huseni turned toward the doorway as a large old man lurched through it. His mahogany skin contrasted with his white pyjamas. Grey hair framed his temples. As he approached, scowling, the major saw that he was the source of the whirring. The jerkiness of his movements and his laboured walk made it obvious that he suffered some disability. He was a cyborg, the first the major had ever seen. That technology had long been abandoned on Earth. The old man glared at the major. Magaly and Huseni looked at each other and shifted uneasily on their feet.

"Dad!" said Zaria, as she came into the room from what the major thought might be the kitchen. The others were behind her. "I thought you'd be in bed by now."

"I was," her father grumbled. "Who's the guy bleeding all over my tiles?"

"Rahim," Magaly ordered, "Go get a paramedic kit and bring some synthaflesh."

"Synthaflesh?" the major snorted. "I didn't know anyone used that any more."

"We don't have your medical technology, Major" Magaly said. "The council has to spend all its foreign exchange on trying to shore up the environmental damage caused by your mining of our moons."

"Put something under his arm before he ruins the furniture," the old man said. Zaria walked up to the major and began to unwind a roll of bandaging. Masika followed with a tray of tinctures and instruments, reminding the major of half-forgotten scenes of the holo-shows he'd seen as a child. As Zaria removed the cloth from around his arm and began to bathe his wound, he turned his face away. He had finally recognized the old man.

"You're Lieutenant Jamal Breiche," he said without looking at him. "Listed as having died in action at the Battle for Basilea."

Zaria's father looked surprised, but Zaria did not seem to be. "You'd be surprised how easy it is to get into the Peacekeepers when your father is a war hero," she said.

Breiche squinted at the major. "How do you know me, Major?"

"I checked out your file. Right after I checked out your daughter's."

"Someone care to tell me what is going on here?" Breiche demanded of the younger people standing silently in the room.

Zaria left the major's side and went over to her father. She had managed to stop the bleeding and had left a dressing loosely draped over his arm. She told him not to move his arm until Rahim had applied the synthaflesh, then led her father out of the front door. The others moved to a corner, where they talked in whispers. The major lay back and closed his eyes, trying to remember what he'd read about Lieutenant Jamal Breiche.

As a bold young lieutenant, Breiche had been credited with leading a small group of Peacekeepers out of a rebel ambush during the war on Basilea over half a century ago. For his courage, he had been awarded a medal of valour in a widely-publicized ceremony and had become a target for rebel assassins, who viewed him as a symbol of Terran oppression. After two unsuccessful attempts on his life, he was hit by sniper fire, then transported off Basilea by a medi-skip and flown to the nearby colony of Palmares, where he had spent two years in treatment, his condition said to be too serious to permit his transfer to Earth, where he would have received better medical care. His condition had never stabilized enough to permit the long journey home, and he had died of his wounds, or perhaps, the record suggested, of incompetent medical treatment. And that was where the official record had ended.

From time to time, rumours sprang up that Breiche was alive and well and living in a Palmaran quilombo. The Terran government dismissed the rumours with the argument that Lieutenant Breiche would have been treated as a war hero back on Earth and therefore would have had no motive for staying away from his young wife, herself a respected high-ranking officer.

One day, a young Palmaran woman applied for Peacekeeper training, invoking her right to the scholarship awarded to the first-generation offspring of Peacekeepers who had served in the colonies. Following confirmation of her parentage by DNA scan, she was admitted. A footnote to Lieutenant Breiche's file said that he had reproduced posthumously, through in-vitro fertilization, or so his daughter, Zaria Breiche, maintained. By then, the Peacekeepers were anxious for fresh recruits; the Terrans had elected a secretary general who was vehemently opposed to conscription, and no one cared that much about a long-dead war hero. Zaria Breiche graduated with honours, served four years on an exploration vessel and then resigned her commission to return to her troubled home planet.

When he had first read the file, he knew it probably told only a fraction of the story. He remembered feeling sorry that she had never known her father, that she had grown up in a society hostile to her half-Terran heritage. Now it was clear that Breiche had not only faked his own death and enlisted several Palmarans to help him cover it up, he was also very deeply involved in political activities which threatened Terran interests. And so was his daughter.

Chapter Fourteen

Zaria had learned long ago to fear that look on her father's face, but not because he was a violent or abusive man. Quite the contrary: Jamal Breiche inspired the deepest respect in his children, and they, in turn, wanted to earn his. It was clear to Zaria that whatever her father was feeling about what she had done, it wasn't respect.

"We had to do something. He was this far from busting the operation at the Aristide."

"I see. So in order to ease his suspicions, you kidnap him and bring him to my house?" Jamal Breiche crossed his arms over his chest and waited for a response.

"Well, no."

"What do you mean 'no'? He's in there now, staining my pallet."

She bit her lip. "It was that or kill him."

Jamal glared at her for a moment. "There were no other options?"

"Well, we considered Sixto's cottage, but that's the first place they'd look."

"I mean there were no other options besides kidnapping or killing him?"

"I didn't have time to think. I had to act quickly."

"I see." He did not look terribly sympathetic. "Well, now that you have him, what are you going to do with him? You don't have a clue, do you?" To Zaria's relief, Sixto and Magaly chose that moment to join them.

"I think we should try to turn him," Sixto suggested. From the look on his face, he was serious.

Magaly's eyebrows arched. "Major Eaglefeather is the chief of security. Rabindra was killed on his orders. He's a senior officer. I don't think he can be convinced to join us."

"Maybe he won't join us," Sixto argued back. "Maybe the best we can hope for is that he won't harm us. That alone would be quite a coup."

"You expect to undo a lifetime of indoctrination? To counteract all he was taught as a Terran and as a Peacekeeper?"

"It's been done before," Sixto maintained. "Jamal here is living proof. And what about Hanif Bjorndahl?"

"Hanif came to us of his own free will, and things have changed since Elder Jamal joined our quilombo. Why would the major join us? He's got everything to lose and nothing to gain."

"He seems to be a moral man."

"How do you know what kind of a man he is? You don't know anything about him!"

"Zaria knows him. Let's find out what she thinks."

All eyes turned to Zaria, who looked thoughtful. "Well ... I don't know him very well. But to reverse Magaly's analysis, we have nothing to lose, and everything to gain if we turn him."

"You're wrong," scowled Magaly. "We have a lot to lose. Our lives."

"What little faith you have in the power of your convictions, young woman," Jamal cut in. The confidence in his voice commanded their instant attention. "You Palmarans maintain that in spite of being technologically behind you are politically and culturally far in advance of the Terrans. If you believe that, it shouldn't be so hard to demonstrate it. If you genuinely believe that the society you've built here is superior, that it truly addresses human needs, then convince the Terran major. I don't think it should be that hard."

Magaly knew she was defeated. "What if it doesn't work? Which it won't. Then what?"

"I have a suggestion," Jamal continued calmly. "Let's put a time limit on this. Let's say two weeks."

"Two weeks!" Sixto protested. "We won't convince him in two weeks."

"Not to convince him," said Jamal, turning away from the others, "to convince

Magaly. If you aren't convinced within two weeks that it might be possible to persuade the major to join us, we can discuss our options at that time."

It was the best Magaly could get under the circumstances. "All right, fine. Go ahead. You have two weeks. But I want some guarantee that after that we will seriously consider all the alternatives, including execution. It's too dangerous to let him live."

Sixto opened his mouth to argue, but Jamal raised a weathered brown hand and cut him off. "Agreed."

Encouraged that Jamal considered her consent key, Magaly continued to place conditions on the agreement. "He has to be under constant guard and physically restrained at all times."

"You may see to it," Jamal agreed.

"Where will he stay?" Zaria asked.

"Here," Jamal replied quickly, "under our roof. I'll take responsibility for looking after his day-to-day needs."

Magaly nodded respectfully at him. "Rahim will stay the night. I'll arrange to have him relieved in the morning." She went back in the house.

Jamal turned his attention to his daughter and Sixto. "I suggest you two continue this discussion and work out a schedule for your major, one that will allow him to become intimately acquainted with our community within two weeks. His life is your responsibility." He then lurched noisily away.

Zaria sighed to herself. Sixto smiled. "Thanks for your backing," he said to Zaria. "May I ask why you had a change of heart?"

She bit her lip. "I couldn't do it. I just couldn't kill him." Were things okay between them now?

"I'm glad to hear it."

Her eyes met his. "I don't know if we did the right thing. This could be a big mistake."

Frowning unsympathetically, he replied, "Well, if it doesn't work, you can always kill him later."

She returned his frown. "I will, if I have to." Perhaps things were not okay.

"I'll go talk to Hanif," he said and left.

That was a good idea. Hanif Bjorndahl's testimony might persuade him. She took a deep breath and went into her parents' house.

Chapter Fifteen

Major Stojic felt ill even before he heard Captain Lobo's report. The captain's arrival meant he would have to put off his plans to visit the Aristide that evening, and now it looked as if his fall-back plan to go there in the morning would also have to be cancelled. His hands were beginning to jerk and his mood was souring fast.

"Did you get a fix on the point of transmission before the signal failed?"

"The cliff overlooking the Tubman village. I can assemble a squad to leave right away." His zeal irritated Major Stojic.

"Contact Palmaran authorities and get permission for a search party to leave Simcoe."

Captain Lobo looked as disappointed as a child denied his favourite dessert. "They'll probably want to escort us. It could take all night!"

"Then it will have to take all night."

"Sir, Major Eaglefeather could be dead by then."

Major Stojic could not muster much concern for the major's safety. He felt edgy and nervous. "He knew the risks. Under the circumstances, he shouldn't have left the compound. Why wasn't I told?"

"It was a security operation, sir," the captain said, as if Major Stojic should understand.

"Yes, I'm sure." Ever since the new major had arrived, Major Stojic had worried that he might somehow upstage him with the colonel. “Major Eaglefeather wanted the glory for himself, didn't he?“

The captain answered with care. “I think he was trying to gather evidence, not to actually apprehend anyone, sir.“

“Well, either way, it was a stupid move. Assemble your team and wait to hear from me.“

“Yes, sir.“ He saluted smartly and left.

As soon as Captain Lobo was gone. Major Stojic tapped out the Aristide's vidphone number. He fidgeted as he counted the beeps till Nailah's face appeared on screen. He could see he had woken her. Her eyes were puffy and her hair mussed. “Nailah?“

“Major Stojic, it's the middle of the night.“

“I'm aware of that. I'm going to be busy all morning. I won't be meeting you at the Aristide.“

“I understand. Major,“ she nodded. “Your package will be waiting for you.“

He tried not to sound desperate. “Yes, but I'm afraid I'm going to be tied up for quite some time. I wonder if you could have one of your people run it over here for me. I'll arrange for payment on receipt of the package.“

“I'll see to it, Major“

Chapter Sixteen

It was just after dawn. White sunlight poured in through the window's billowing yellow curtains. The major was weak and exhausted. A fuzzy warmth in the crook of his arm made him look down. A wee puppy nestled there, curled up asleep, its tiny chest gently rising and sinking with its breathing. In the distance, he could hear children playing. The window in his room must be open, he thought, but he was too tired to get out of bed to close it.

The shouting and laughter woke the puppy. Its little head popped up and its big brown eyes blinked at the major. He patted its head, but that only made it more alert. The shouts of the children outside grew louder. The puppy rose on unsteady legs and jumped to the floor. It yipped and jumped futilely at the window until, as the major watched in astonishment, it began to grow rapidly before his eyes. Within seconds it had become a Malamute with thick grey fur, its bark deepening malevolently.

The dog turned from the window and growled at him. I'd better get out of here, he said to himself. He slowly began to ease himself towards the far side of the bed, hoping to roll off, then steal away without alarming the animal. Then he felt a sharp pain in his right forearm. He jerked back to find the dog's teeth sunk in his flesh.

Eaglefeather cried out and sat bolt upright on the recliner in which he had been sleeping, and to which his left hand was cuffed. He found himself looking at the weathered brown face of the old man, who was sitting across from him.

Shaken, it took him a moment to remember that he was in former Lieutenant Jamal Breiche's house in the quilombo of Tubman. His bandaged wound still throbbed. He looked down to see a metaplastic model of a shuttle in his lap, and realized that it had hit him in his sore arm and woken him up. The man with the earring, Rahim, came from behind the recliner and removed the toy from the major's lap. He tossed it back to a group of young girls; one caught it gratefully out of the air and they ran off.

It was daylight, the major realized groggily, and he could see his surroundings much more clearly now. The back of the Breiche home faced onto a small green space surrounded by others of similar size and design. There was a little playground at the far end of the field, complete with a slide and sandbox. A young girl dashed up the slide and slid down with loud whoops.

Although the pain in his arm was fading, waves of fatigue and nausea washed over him. He fought to hide his symptoms from his guards but had to admit to himself that he did not feel at all well. He fell back on the recliner

“Are you all right?“ Breiche asked. His eyes looked worried.

“You must enjoy hearing those little cherubs first thing every morning,“ the major said in a hoarse voice.

“I love the sound of children playing, Major,“ the old man replied, his eyes stony. “We Palmarans are a child-loving people.“

“Obviously, since you seem to have more than you can afford.“

“You would begrudge us even our children, Major?“ The old man sounded annoyed, but the major went on.

“Well, curtailing your population growth would help halt the environmental degradation you people complain about. This planet could easily sustain a population of about half its current size.“ He was surprised at his own belligerence. He was not himself, but he didn't care.

“It will sustain no life at all if the mining continues at its current rate,“ the old man retorted. “You Terrans would deny us our right to have the children we want, rather than cut back on your own energy consumption. You have the highest per capita rate of quilidon consumption in the galaxy. Major, if your people weren't so wasteful, you wouldn't need to mine our moons and our planet would stabilize."

"My people! You're Terran too, Lieutenant. What about your responsibilities to your own people? Why don't you go home and tell it to them? I'm sure they'd find a deserter's version of the conflict here extremely enlightening."

That riled the old man. "Ah, yes," he said. "Now I understand. I'd forgotten how Peacekeepers are indoctrinated into believing that desertion is the worst of all possible crimes."

"And what would you call leaving your troops in the midst of battle?"

"For your information, Major, I was wounded very early in the war. I was taken out on a hospital skip that stopped here so that the critically wounded, including me, could be treated. I spent six months in a hospital in this quilombo. It was here I learned I would never walk on my own legs again. It was here that I met my wife, Nailah. Given the choice of going back to Earth, getting patched up and returned to the front, I decided to stay here. I had that right."With what appeared to be a great effort he rose from his chair, oblivious to the whirring that produced, and staggered clumsily into the house.

After he had gone, the major noticed Rahim sitting on a bench nearby, reading quietly. "Feisty old man," the major remarked.

The young man looked up from his technical manual. "We refer to him as an Elder."

The major regretted his comment, but not for long. He had no reason to feel sorry. Being held against his will made for a rather good reason to forget his manners. Still, it wasn't smart to antagonize his captors. He should be studying his surroundings and working on an escape plan. If he talked to his captors at all, it should be to get information and to win their sympathy. He was being held in a residential area, easy enough to attract attention, he thought. Should he cry for help? It would take his guard at least a few seconds to react. A few seconds might be enough. But suppose someone came? What would happen once they noticed his black uniform?

Rahim looked up. He turned his handpad off and set it aside. “Now that you're awake, let's go through the rules, shall we, Major? First, you have some choices to make. You can choose to live or you can choose to die. Second, you can spend your days here with us conscious or unconscious. Take your pick.“

Footsteps sounded behind him. With effort, the major half-turned and saw Zaria walk through the doorway. She was wearing a mid-calf-length dress today, with brown and orange batiked designs, loose and airy. Seeing her brought back his dream and the memory of her betrayal. He had once felt for Zaria what he'd felt for the helpless puppy, but like the Malamute in his dream, she had betrayed him, and she had deliberately and maliciously hurt him.

“How is your arm healing. Major?“ she asked pleasantly.

“It itches.“

“Itching is a good sign,“ Rahim said. “I must be going, Zaria. I have three skips to repair by tomorrow. Huseni should be here by now, but he isn't. Do you mind?“

“No, go ahead. I'll stay. Sixto will be back in a while, anyway.“

Rahim quickly gathered his manuals and departed. Zaria seated herself on the bench he had vacated. The major did not feel like being cordial, though he knew he had to treat her as he would his other captors. He had his objectives and he had to pursue them.

“Are you prepared to kill me if I try to escape?“ he brought himself to ask.

“I hope you're not planning on trying to escape, Major. You won't get far.“

“Am I ever going to be allowed to leave?“

“I don't know,“ she said, not meeting his eyes.

She doesn't want to kill me, he reminded himself.

“I won't provide you with information,“ he told her. “And as for my value as a hostage, the Peacekeepers will consider me quite expendable. Eventually, you will have to kill me.“

“I hope that won't be necessary.“

"You really had me right here," he said, pointing to the palm of his hand. "Masika's lover. I sure can pick my allies."

"I know you're angry now," she replied, her brown eyes large as they caught his again. "But try to understand us. Keep an open mind."

He laughed bitterly. "You kidnap me, slice up my arm, fake my death — and now you want me to try to understand you?"

She looked troubled. "Major, you once told me you wanted to help bring peace to Palmares."

"And you told me I was naive. You were right."

"I'm sorry it was necessary to lie to you. Are you going to let your anger with me stop you from accomplishing what you want to do here?"

"And what would that be?"

"You say you want peace. I think you're a man of integrity. But if you want to help bring peace to Palmares, you're going to have to forget what you've learned in the Peacekeepers about Palmares. You're going to have to change how you look at things."

He closed his eyes for a moment. "I was quite prepared to forget much of what I had heard about Palmarans, Zaria. Prepared to trust my own impressions. Look where it got me."

Tears welled in her eyes. He heard footsteps on the path. "Please," she implored, "don't make us kill you."

Sixto Masika stepped onto the patio. Zaria went to greet him. "Where is Hanif?"

"He wouldn't come," Masika whispered, looking disappointed.

Zaria lowered her head. "What now?"

"I guess we're on our own, for now."

"I have to go to the wedding today," Zaria told him. "Rahim left, and Huseni is supposed to be here, but he hasn't come yet. Can you stay?"

"What wedding?"

"Jung-Min and Priya. I agreed to perform. I really have to go."

"Yes, well, I have a lecture later this morning. I suppose I could skip it."

"No," Zaria said, "you'd better not depart from your normal

routine. Carry on as usual. I'll go hunt someone up to take over."

The major wanted to laugh. "Well, I'm absolutely overwhelmed with the efficiency of your organization. You take prisoners without the slightest idea of how you intend to hold them." Zaria swept out of the room without responding. "Which one of you is in charge of this crack team, anyway?"

"Unlike the Peacekeepers, we don't have authoritarian leadership," Masika said proudly.

"Who makes decisions?" the major asked. His life might depend on the answer.

"Some of us are designated. We just talk till we agree."

"And if you don't agree?"

"We work it out."

"And this is how you intend to decide what to do with me?"

Masika sucked in a deep breath. "If you'd studied your history, you'd know that many Terran societies have not seen fit to put important decisions in the hands of self-serving politicians and generals."

"And what societies would these be?"

Masika smiled. "Funny you should ask. Many of the First Nations of the Americas had systems of government that were far more democratic than anything we know today. The nations of the Iroquois Confederation, for example, knew the true meaning of consensus."

The major knew that, but he was wary of historical interpretations used to defend injustice. "My ancestors' indecision, superstitions, and inability to join forces were their downfall. We were our own worst enemy. That's why we were conquered, why we spent centuries fighting extinction."

"Yes," Masika agreed, "military conquest has rendered many a culture extinct, but we believe in learning from history, Major, and Terran history is rich and diverse. Many values long forgotten there still matter to us. But you Terrans can't seem to respect that."

"You haven't exactly gone out of your way to earn my respect."

Surprisingly, the young Black man nodded in agreement. “I understand that, Major. I'm truly sorry for the way you've been treated. Even our desperation cannot excuse some of our actions. But sometimes it's hard to know the correct course of action, and even when you know you've done the right thing, you have to wonder whether it will make any difference in the end.“

The major was not in a mood to sympathize. “Sorry to have caused you such a moral dilemma. You can always resolve it by letting me go.“

Masika smiled but said nothing.

The sixteen troopers Captain Einar Lobo had hand-picked had been waiting all night and most of the morning for permission from the Palmaran Governing Council in Imhotep to enter Tubman and search for the missing major. When permission had at last been granted, they'd had to wait for the Palmaran escort they'd been assigned, a man in his sixties called Tazio. Now, the captain found himself held up by his own commanding officer, Major Stojic. The major had given no specific reason for requiring him and his contingent to wait. He'd simply said that he needed to attend to some urgent business before they left.

As the captain had heard from veterans of the war on Basilea, waiting was the hardest thing Peacekeepers could be asked to do. It allowed them to think too much, to imagine the worst, exhausting their energies before they saw any action at all. Beside himself with impatience, he strode to Major Stojic's office, prepared to threaten to go Colonel Welch if the order to move out were not issued immediately. But the moment he saw the major, he knew something was terribly wrong with him.

Major Stojic was pale and soaking in his own perspiration. His bloodshot eyes watered and his nose was running profusely. As the captain began his argument for immediate departure, he could see that Major Stojic was preoccupied, continually glancing at his wrist chronometer, comparing its readings to the one on the wall.

One unsteady hand kept mopping his forehead, eyes, and nose. Captain Lobo was on the verge of calling the chief medical officer when the buzzer sounded. Major Stojic depressed the button that opened his office door.

One of the most beautiful women Lobo had ever seen glided into the office. She was clothed in a green parasilk sari, her long black hair flowing loose down her back. She carried a small package under her arm.

"Ah, Persis, my dear" Major Stojic fawned, putting his arm around her shoulder and lifting the package quickly from her hands. "I've been waiting for hours. I'll be with you in just a minute." He turned to Captain Lobo. "Captain, you're dismissed.

Captain Lobo left in disgust. Major Stojic's addiction to bliss had long been a subject of gossip within the compound. The captain had had little interest in the matter — as far as he had known, the major's off-duty activities had had no impact on his performance as an officer, but this was different. He would raise the matter with Colonel Welch at the first opportunity.

Chapter Seventeen

People were gathering at Merae Goree, each arrival bringing a contribution to the feast they would share after the ceremony. It was sunny and bright, a day so normal on Palmares it was almost boring, but the weather on a day such as this should not be taken for granted, Zaria reminded herself.

The white robe she wore was trimmed with a Kente design. Beneath it was the dance costume she would wear for her performance that afternoon. She felt elegant, honoured to be entertaining at the ceremony. The ceremony's convenor, Tuyet Chowdhury, had never looked more beautiful. Tuyet, a slender woman with a single waist-length grey braid that swung like a pendulum when she walked, wore a delicately-embroidered red parasilk tunic over her white pants. The two women who would commit themselves in marriage today, Jung-Min Behr and Priya Said, had chosen well.

As Zaria set up the holo-imager to project the images of the percussionists who would accompany her dance, she caught herself imagining her own wedding. In times past, the groom had been a shapeless apparition. Lately, though, he'd looked more and more like Sixto Masika. A group of children ran past, nearly sending the holo-imager crashing to the ground. "Sorry!" they laughed and ran on. The sight made her long for a life in which children could thrive, but the idea of marriage and family was so remote that it seemed almost not worth thinking about.

Her reverie was broken by the approach of Magaly Uxmal,

looking almost childlike in an oversized huipile as colourful as those worn when the Mayans flourished. The sight awakened Zaria's earliest memories of her childhood friend.

In the beginning, every child in the class had sympathized with little Magaly Uxmal. She was a frail-looking girl and they wanted to protect her, even more so when they learned she did not speak. The poor girl had lost both her parents in a flood and, having no other family, she had been adopted by a local couple. The teacher had urged everyone to be patient with Magaly. She was in therapy and maybe, someday, would talk. Their sympathy and compassion had quickly waned, for despite their best efforts, Magaly wanted nothing to do with them. She would not join in their games, sit next to anyone or share lunch. No one could persuade her to utter a sound. After a while, they gave up on her.

Standing apart from the other children was something Zaria and Magaly had in common. The two girls slowly came to share a wordless solidarity. They sat side by side, then played together and walked home together, arm in arm. The teachers were gratified to see their friendship flower. Zaria chattered incessantly and Magaly listened or didn't. No one, including Zaria, could ever really tell.

One afternoon, a group of boys blocked their path. They took turns teasing Magaly about her silence. Zaria, large for her age, stepped in front of her friend and shouted at the boys to let them pass. Emboldened by their numbers, the boys turned on Zaria and taunted her with shouts that her mother was a Terrafucker and that she was a half-Terran mutant. Having lost her fear of fighting long ago, Zaria plowed into them. The boys had expected this and were prepared. What they were not prepared for, however, was Magaly's response. Screaming "STOP!" at the top of her voice, she had followed her only friend into battle. After a few wild punches, the boys began to quarrel among themselves about the wisdom of fighting with the pathetic Magaly. At the same time, they found her windmill-style of fighting difficult to defend against. They ran off, leaving the two girls quivering in fury. Magaly talked readily after that, mostly to Zaria.

*

Tuyet Chowdhury was calling the guests together under the shade of the thatched canopy. The ceremony would soon begin. Zaria walked over to Magaly and stood beside her. Almost a head shorter than her friend, Magaly looked up and smiled. To Zaria it signalled a temporary respite from the strain and it felt good.

"How is our friend doing?" Magaly whispered. "Ready to defect yet?"

"It might interest you to know that I've thought of a way out of this that will satisfy both you and Sixto."

"Oh?"

"Ever considered a prisoner exchange?" The idea had come to Zaria last night. According to information Persis had come by weeks ago, a prisoner transport would soon be stopping to pick up Palmarans destined for the Jovian asteroid belt. Two captured Kituhwa were among those to be taken away.

A slow smile spread across Magaly's face. "Not bad," she said, not the least distracted by the ceremony's commencement. "Not bad at all. We should talk, after this."

Jung-Min and Priya, their hands joined, stood before Tuyet in the centre of a circle formed by the celebrants. Zaria marvelled that she could be taking part in something as wholesome, as ordinary, as a wedding. Even if the major were to join the Kituhwa — which was unlikely — her life would never be the same and she would never be able to forgive herself for the injury she had done him. By the time Zaria turned her thoughts back to the ceremony, Jung-Min was concluding the vows she had written to her lover: "Loving you has made me a better person. I look forward to loving you for the rest of my life."

The newlyweds embraced and kissed, to the applause of the guests. Then, with the convenor, they joined hands and bowed their heads in meditation. The celebrants fell silent till Tuyet's strong voice rang out in song. Some guests earnestly chimed in, Magaly among them. The beautiful harmonies lingered in Zaria's ears long after the final note.

"Jung-Min and Priya," Tuyet declared, "we are honoured that you have asked us to witness your vows to love and stand by each other for the rest of your lives. We accept our responsibility to you, for when two people join in marriage, their families and friends are also joined through them. We accept and stand by your commitment to each other."

She spread her arms as if to beckon all of Palmares. "Let us celebrate this union of two people and the strength it gives our quilombo. Let us feast, for we have each contributed to this celebration. Let our feast remind us that each person's contribution to the quilombo is unique, welcome, and essential."

To Jung-Min and Priya she said, "Our blessing upon you both, my daughters." She embraced them, signifying the end of the ceremony.

The circle broke apart. Zaria and Magaly waited their turn to congratulate the two women. A child was heard asking his mother impatiently, "Can we eat now?"

Magaly moved to congratulate the newlyweds. She hugged and kissed Priya. Zaria heard Priya say softly in Magaly's ear: "There's a wrecked skip at the bottom of the cliff. Do you know about it?"

"I'm aware of it," Magaly replied.

"Should I be worried?"

"No, you should be happy and looking forward to sharing the rest of your life with Jung-Min." The two women hugged again. Zaria smiled encouragingly at them, but they took little notice.

The celebrants greeted Zaria's performance with generous warmth. It was so different than performing for off-worlders. While Palmarans were more appreciative of and knowledgeable about the dances and music, they also had higher expectations. They were unimpressed by bright colours, erotic movements, and loud drumming. They appreciated grace, precision, and respect for form. She felt a special satisfaction and pride.

It was not till she pulled her robe over her costume after her performance that Zaria heard the low humming of stratoskips. The chatter and laughter stopped as more and more people turned and pointed at the sky in the east.

Four skips circled them from above. Each bore the Peacekeeper's emblem, a white dove in an orange circle. The roar of their engines caused the ground to vibrate. Crying broke out among the younger children. After a U-turn, the lead skip landed on top of the Merae, flattening a good section of the garden. Zaria knew it was no accident.

The wedding guests backed away from the skip and from the Peacekeepers leaping from it. Zaria moved forward. Out of the corner of her eye, she saw Magaly moving in the same direction. Tuyet, however, was a few steps ahead of both of them. As the only elder present and the Convenor of Ceremonies, she would be the first to greet the Peacekeepers. Zaria knew Major Stojic from the Aristide, but the captain standing beside him was a stranger. The Palmaran official who accompanied them wore a mediator's armband.

With effort, Tuyet addressed the Palmaran official over the noise of the three skips hovering just off the cliff. "You are interrupting a wedding." Magaly and Zaria stood just behind her.

"Sorry, but we have an emergency situation here," the Palmaran responded politely. He introduced himself as Mediator Tazio, but before he could explain why they were there, he was interrupted by the Peacekeeper wearing a captain's insignia.

"Didn't any of you notice that stratoskip at the foot of the cliff?"

"We noticed," Tuyet said uncertainly.

"And none of you bothered to report it?" the captain asked, his face turning pink.

Magaly answered, matching his hostility. "Our communications are being jammed, Captain. Besides, how were we to know when it crashed?"

"The explosion might have given you a hint."

"The cliff shields our village from noise on this side of the mountain," Tuyet calmly explained. "No one would have heard it crash unless they were here on Merae Goree." Zaria was glad the elder was there to respond. Because Tuyet had no involvement in the Kituhwa, she would be neither defensive nor hostile.

"Right," he said skeptically.

Mediator Tazio intervened. "Let me handle this, Captain, if you please." He addressed Tuyet again. "I'm afraid I'm going to have to ask your group to leave. We're investigating the crash site and looking for possible survivors."

"Has this been approved by the Governing Council in Imhotep?" Tuyet asked.

"Yes, Elder." The mediator was respectful. "I'm sorry. Perhaps you can continue your celebration in the quilombo."

Major Stojic, although technically not in command on Palmaran territory, took charge. "And if there is anyone with information that might help us out, there's a reward." Zaria saw the look of pure disgust that the captain shot at the oblivious major.

"I will spread the word, Major," Tuyet assured him. She strode back to the wedding party to deliver the news. Magaly, however, seemed rooted there, so Zaria stayed. Major Stojic greeted Zaria, apparently noticing her for the first time. In the background she heard disapproving groans. She knew it was unlikely the celebration would continue elsewhere after the work of cleaning up.

"Do you need any assistance?" Magaly asked Major Stojic. The offer surprised Zaria. Whatever Magaly was up to, she hoped it would not put them in further jeopardy.

"Assistance of what nature, young lady?" the major said, looking her up and down.

Magaly sounded like an innocent school girl. "Well, my friends and I know this area quite well. We could help you search for the pilot and any survivors."

The captain spoke up quickly. "I'm sure that won't be —"

"Splendid idea," Major Stojic interrupted. "We could indeed use your help, just this way, if you please." He led Magaly toward the skip. The mediator followed obligingly.

The captain stood stiffly, watching their departing backs. Then, suddenly aware that Zaria was watching him, he turned on his heel and followed Major Stojic without a word.

Chapter Eighteen

"Go ahead, Major," Jamal Breiche urged good-naturedly. "It's good food. Won't hurt you."

The major's reluctance had not been based on fear. He simply lacked an appetite. But he needed to keep up his strength, so he ate.

"I remember when I first came here," Breiche said. "Couldn't find meat anywhere. I would have killed for a lousy hamburger. After a while I got used to it, even felt a bit better."

Breiche was waiting for someone to relieve him of his post. Huseni had come but had left almost immediately, leaving the major alone with Breiche. His captors were not worried that he might escape, not wounded and chained.

A boy of about seven years, his skin the colour of milk chocolate, was walking towards them from the square. Breiche, facing the major, could not see him. The major said nothing, hoping that the child's curiosity might lead to something that would help him. It was only after the boy's steps sounded on the tiles that Breiche turned around to greet him.

"Elder Jamal?" the boy said timidly. Breiche looked uneasy to find him there. "Joachim, my boy. What are you doing here?"

The child's eyes fixed on the major. "My mother said to come here to make sure you were all right. You didn't come to the garden this morning. You were going to show me how to plant hargots today, remember?"

"I'm sorry, Joachim. I forgot. I've been very busy. Can we do it tomorrow?"

"That's okay. Tomorrow's okay. Who's he?" He pointed at the major, who was enjoying Breiche's discomfort

"He's my visitor, Joachim. You must run along now."

"He's a Peacekeeper, Elder," the boy observed. "Is he a bad man? Is he going to hurt you?"

"No, he's not going to hurt me."

It angered the major that the boy had been taught to fear Peacekeepers. He supposed Palmaran parents were passing on their distrust to their children, ensuring the continuation of hostilities for another generation.

"Are you going to kill him?" Joachim asked.

Breiche looked genuinely alarmed. "No, Joachim, I'm not going to kill him. Killing is a terrible thing to do. I don't kill people. Here take this." From a bowl on the end table, he handed the child a fruit. "Go home now. And don't tell anyone you saw this man here. We don't want to scare anyone."

"Okay, Elder. See you tomorrow." Joachim ran off toward the playground, where a young woman sat on a bench. She waved in their direction, and Breiche returned her wave.

"Aren't you worried that he'll tell everyone in the quilombo?" the major asked.

"Not at all. This is the family home of a former Peacekeeper and a woman who is believed to be a collaborator. We have entertained Peacekeepers and Consortium executives here on occasion. Most people don't know what Nailah and I are up to and don't want to know."

"You lied to him. About killing me, I mean."

"If you get killed here, it won't be by my hand. I gave up killing long ago."

"Sure. Now you just chain people and complain when they bleed too much."

That was the pattern their conversation had taken all day. The major would say something insulting, and Breiche would leave him alone for a while. This time, when Breiche tried to leave, he caught his foot in a recess in a low bench. Frustrated, he knocked the bench over, trying to untangle himself. The major couldn't help him, since he was chained, but he wasn't sure he would have bothered anyway.

"That neuro-stim implant must be quite the handicap," he said, after Breiche had disentangled himself. "I've never seen one in use before, outside a museum that is. Spinal injuries can be treated these days. You'd be walking normally if you'd gone back to Earth."

"Yes, I remember the routine. Patch them up as quickly as possible and ship them back to the front."

"Freedom comes with a price, Lieutenant."

Breiche laughed bitterly. "Oh, I know that. Major. I'm freer than I have ever been, and the price was high indeed. I let my family and friends back on Earth believe I was dead, but I've never regretted it. I have more here on Palmares than I could have ever hoped to have had on Earth. And since the day I came here, you're the first person who's called my walking difficulty a handicap." He left, this time without incident. He was gone for a long time.

It was getting dim. People were disappearing from the fields. The major felt better, and now that he had a meal in his stomach, he wanted to stand, to stretch, to walk, but he was still chained. Mental exercise was the only kind he was likely to get, so he went over the conversations he'd had with his captors, hoping to recall something that might be useful. There wasn't much, but Breiche had said something significant. A plan began to form in his mind. It was a simple plan, because he had only one guard, but it depended on the old man's return. He was taking a long time and the major would have to move quickly. He wished he hadn't insulted the old man. He should have encouraged him to stay, kept him talking.

"Lieutenant!" he called into the house. "Lieutenant Breiche!" He called several times before Breiche appeared in the doorway.

"I have to relieve myself," the major told him.

The old man remained still, his face expressionless.

"Are you going to unchain me or do I have to further damage

your furniture?"

"You'd only have to sit in it."

For a moment, he thought the old man was going to turn and go back into the house. But then he pulled a narrow, thin electronic key from under his loose fitting shirt and tossed it to the major. "Here."

Breiche reached under his shirt again, and this time his hand emerged holding a weapon. The major was on his feet by then, but he froze as Breiche pointed it at him.

"Not so fast," the old man said. He tossed the major a pair of handcuffs. They looked like museum pieces. "Put these on. So your hands are cuffed together."

It did not necessarily jeopardize his plan. He complied quickly, his adrenaline beginning to flow.

"Now toss me back the key," Breiche instructed.

Again, the major complied—but instead of a toss, he managed a strong pitch right at the old man's head.

Breiche ducked quickly, lost his balance and fell. By the time he had struggled into a sitting position, the major was on the run.

"Stop," Breiche called out. Glancing back, the major saw that he had guessed correctly. Breiche was no longer aiming the weapon at him. There was no point. He was out of stun range by now. The old man simply watched him go.

He had counted on the horror in Breiche's voice when the child had asked if he were going to kill him: "Killing is a terrible thing... I don't kill people." It had sounded sincere, and it was. His weapon had been set to stun and would stay there.

Having no idea of the quilombo's layout, the major kept close to cover, hoping to determine his whereabouts later. As he turned from the courtyard and down an alley between two large houses, he saw a flurry of activity in the near distance. In despair, he recognized the woman running rapidly toward him as Magaly Uxmal. She was yelling and waving her arms wildly, signalling to Keoki, on the other side of the field.

As she approached, he saw the weapon she was aiming at him. He froze, knowing that it had the range to kill him instantly and that, unlike Breiche, she would not hesitate. As she shot at him, he raised his cuffed hands in the universal signal for surrender and dove, head first, into the dirt. She fired at him again on his way down.

"Don't shoot!" he called out. "I give up!"

She slowed to a quick walk and came up to him without lowering her weapon. "Jamal, are you all right?" she barked, without so much as a look at the old man, who was advancing as rapidly as his neuro-stim would allow.

"I'm fine, child." The old man's voice was calm. "No need to hurt him."

"Magaly, don't!" cried another man, running towards them. "Don't kill him!" The major looked up and saw Masika and Zaria following Breiche and winced at the irony. Moments ago, he had been alone, trying to get Breiche's attention.

"He was trying to escape," Magaly said. "He was your responsibility, Sixto. What happened?"

"Relax. He didn't get away. I had to leave him with Jamal to go to teach my class."

"Well, between the two of you I'm surprised he's not back to the base by now." She sounded dangerously angry. "Get up! Get back to the cottage!" It took him a moment to understand that she was not going to shoot again, that she was ordering him to move.

"Zaria," Magaly ordered when they returned, "chain him to the pillar."

He paid little attention as Breiche passed the key to his daughter. He felt oddly comforted by the familiar scent of Zaria's perfume as she leaned over him to lock the chain.

While Magaly was demanding an explanation, the major gained control of his breathing. Masika and Breiche took turns trying to calm her, but Magaly would have none of it. "Look," she bellowed, waving her weapon about wildly, "I want either Keoki, Huseni or Rahim here with this guy at all times. Understand? You two men couldn't be trusted to step on a cockroach."

"Magaly, just calm down," Masika ordered. "No harm has been done."

Zaria ignored her comrades and unwrapped the major's bandages to check on his wound. After a while, Magaly bolstered her weapon. Breiche went for tea. Night began to settle. The major's captors relaxed in the cool night air.

Magaly sipped her mate, then turned to the major. "You may be interested in knowing that you're officially listed as dead, Major. The investigation at the crash site concluded you that your body must have fallen into the sea. No one is looking for you."

Wondering how she knew that, the major considered the implications. Now that he had botched one escape, future attempts would be far more difficult, and if she were telling the truth, he could no longer hope to be rescued. When Zaria left the patio with her father, the major felt abandoned and depressed.

o

Although Colonel Welch had been gracious enough to see him, it was clear to Captain Lobo that he considered the visit unwelcome. Good manager that he was, the colonel thought it inadvisable to show a lack of faith in the two majors by meeting with their subordinates. However, given that Major Eaglefeather was missing and presumed dead and that Captain Lobo had worked closely with him, the colonel had decided to see him, just this once.

The captain's zeal meant he was only slightly discouraged by the colonel's gruff interruption. "We've known for some time that Major Stojic is an addict, Captain. It's not news."

"Yes, sir, but it's beginning to interfere with the performance of his duties, sir"

Now the colonel was paying attention. "In what way?"

"He delayed our search of the crash site this morning, waiting for a drug delivery."

"Did he?" The colonel's eyebrows went up.

"Yes, sir. I also believe his judgment is impaired. He utilized Palmaran civilians to help with the search for Major Eaglefeather."

"I see." The colonel stroked his chin. "Are your findings

suspect? Is it possible Major Eaglefeather is still alive?"

"I don't think so, sir. It's probable that the body washed out to sea. The current in that area is pretty strong. We're searching, but we have to face the fact that it may never turn up. His homing device would have short-circuited in the water. The problem is..." the captain hesitated, looking for words that would not make him look like he was vying for promotion.

The colonel lost patience again. "What, Captain? Spit it out!"

"Sir, you know that Major Eaglefeather thought that someone here on the base is providing information to the Palmarans."

"Yes, and I concur with the major's suspicions."

"Sir, this is going to sound rather far-fetched, but I think that Major Stojic is our leak."

"Major Stojic? He's been stationed here for eight years. Spotless record."

"He's an addict, sir. Spends most of his free time at the Aristide. That place is notorious for drug trafficking. I think he might be trading information for Bliss."

"An interesting theory." The colonel seemed to be thinking about it.

"Even if I'm wrong, sir, Major Stojic is hardly the officer he once was. His lack of judgment in using Palmaran civilians to help in the search proves it. He should be relieved of duty."

"Perhaps, Captain." The colonel looked thoughtful. "If you're correct. Major Stojic may be able to provide us with the evidence we need to get Masika."

Captain Lobo nodded slowly, wondering if the colonel really believed him or simply found his accusation convenient.

Chapter Nineteen

Keoki was not a quiet man, but Breiche seemed happy with the company. Now inside the house, the major had been listening for hours as the two discussed the melancholic music playing on the holo-imager and drank mate from straw-like metal tubes.

Eventually, Keoki suggested that the major might want a shower, and he said that he would. Keoki led him upstairs, still chained. Once unchained, the major undressed and showered. Keoki stood unobtrusively nearby, studying something on a handpad. The major decided that if any of his captors could be encouraged to talk, it would be Keoki.

"What do you do for a living, Keoki? Besides sabotage and kidnapping, I mean."

"Actually, I'm an architect," Keoki said good-naturedly.

The major was surprised. "Really? That must be very interesting."

"I think so."

"I imagine there's no shortage of work, either. What with your rapid population growth and all."

"That's true, the young man replied, "although most of my contracts lately have been to renovate buildings to shore them up against quakes and tremors."

"Must be quite the challenge on a planet as geologically unstable as this is."

"Yes, we've made dramatic advances in designing quake-resistant structures. But it's rather a futile exercise."

As the water ran over his body, the major looked out the

window and down on the hexagonal courtyard below. The Aristide was also hexagonal and, though he had not seen much of Tubman quilombo, the major had the impression that it too was made up of hexagons. He asked Keoki about it.

The six-sided design predominated simply because a single group of architects had designed the original settlements, Keoki told him. "But it does foster the development of community, at least in our quilombo."

"How so?"

"Well, contrast it with the way many Terran cities were designed, especially following the invention of the automobile: a tic-tac-toe arrangement of filing cabinets, with cars given priority access to every building. Here, we put our roads around the plazas. That way, groundskips don't intrude on our daily activities. Each plaza is a small self-contained community. Buildings face each other. You can't leave your building without facing a neighbouring one, no matter which way you turn. And everyone has equal access to recreation, usually a park at the centre."

Eaglefeather nodded. He understood that the design promoted community. He also realized that the topic of conversation they had happened upon was fortuitous.

"I don't really get it," he said, climbing out of the shower and drying himself off. "It's kind of hard to visualize. And it doesn't sound very convenient."

"It's not necessarily convenient for travelling," Keoki admitted. "It encourages walking, and groundskips are usually inconvenienced, but it's healthy."

"What about moving large goods around?" The major began to dress. "Like furniture, appliances, building materials..."

"Groundskips, like everywhere else."

"So groundskips have access to each building in each plaza?" Eaglefeather asked stupidly. "And the plazas are connected?"

Under the impression that he was not making much headway with a verbal description of the quilombo plan, Keoki tapped at his handpad and allowed Eaglefeather to consider the graphic display that was called up.

Still shirtless, the major took the handpad and studied the map. Keeping his mouth in a symbolic zero-shape to project innocent curiosity, he punched up other graphic samples. Keoki continued explaining the design concepts, while Eaglefeather feigned interest. In the meantime, he committed much of Tubman's layout to memory. He would have a direction in mind for his next escape.

They returned to the main room just as Masika arrived with a holo-cube the group had been waiting to see. While his captors laughed, joked and gossiped about people on the cube, the major had a clear view of the little figures attending the wedding of Priya and Jung-Min. As he watched, he felt himself warming to the Palmaran people once more. The enthusiasm, respect and interest he'd had upon his arrival was slowly returning. He reminded himself that his bitterness was recent, the result of his treatment at the hands of only a few wrong-headed people, and he admonished himself for losing touch with the values he held so strongly.

Watching Zaria's perform for her people, seeing her happy, gracious and caring, stirred him. "When are you going to marry my daughter?" Breiche asked. For the briefest moment, the major thought the old man was addressing him.

"We haven't discussed it yet," said Masika. "We've talked about having kids, though. I'm happy to announce you can expect at least six grandchildren."

"They always say that before the first one," Breiche said. "But, seriously, you could make it a double wedding. With Tariq and Persis."

"It's not a good time to marry, Jamal. Not until we settle this business."

"Every generation says that. There is never a good time, never a time free from war and tragedy. It's just part of being human." Masika only nodded and sipped at his mate.

When the cube ended and Keoki turned the music on again, the major occupied himself by quietly performing isometric exercises.

Chapter Twenty

The shuttle took off again into the hazy purple night a few minutes after Zaria hopped off. She had been among the half-dozen people the public vehicle had delivered to the launch pad just inside the compound's ruined wall. She shoved her identidisc into a slot and waited for it to confirm her status as a permanent resident of Simcoe and signal the security gate to slide open and allow her passage. As it closed behind her, Zaria let herself relax.

The scan had been routine, but as was the case with most technology, the Identiscan sometimes malfunctioned. Once, she had been among the unlucky shuttle passengers detained in a special windowless room. They had spent most of the day there, sitting on a hard bench awaiting clearance. The absence of conversation had been awkward: six of them in a small room, afraid that talking with a stranger would implicate them in some wrongdoing if that stranger did not pass muster. The Peacekeeper on duty had taken his time, sending them one by one into another featureless room for questioning. A young boy had been questioned separately from his mother.

That day Zaria had recalled the stories she'd heard about what happened to captured Kituhwa. It would be better to be killed in action than arrested and interrogated. That time, her group of passengers had been cleared.

Zaria walked slowly, less from fatigue than from the strain of the past day, strain that was not about to let up. On returning to the Aristide, her first order of business would be to check with

Persis about the prisoner transport. They needed to know exactly when it was due and who was scheduled to depart on it. Then they would have to think up some way of contacting Colonel Welch, to make their offer of a trade. With effort, she gave up the idea of relaxing in a bath and then crawling into bed. She had no time for that.

It wasn't until she began her climb up the hill to the Aristide that she noticed the quiet. The club was still and dark, at a time when it should be bustling with activity. She ran the last few steps. She could think of many reasons for the club being empty and none of them were good.

Nailah, Tariq and Persis were sitting around a table in grim conversation. Maintenance droids buzzed purposefully about, masking the sound of Zaria's footsteps on the tile. She was almost at the table before her mother noticed her.

Relief washed over Nailah's face as she called out Zaria's name and rushed to embrace her. "Thank the Goddess, you're back," she murmured into her daughter's hair.

Zaria was shocked by her mother's emotional greeting. "What's going on here? Why are we closed up?"

"We're not opening tonight," Persis said. "Haven't you heard?" Zaria stared blankly at her.

"They're expecting a quake," Tariq explained. "Here. The epicentre is just off the coast. The Consortium predicted it will come in the next two hours."

"Two hours! We never heard anything in Tubman. When did they announce it?"

Tariq looked puzzled and worried. "This morning."

"I was afraid of that." Nailah looked even more worried than her son. "Communications are still blacked out. Even the comnet is down."

"Surely they would lift it for news like this," said Persis.

"We never heard," Zaria repeated adamantly. "No one knows. They're going about business as usual in the quilombo."

As she spoke the words, she shivered. Palmaran quakes were deadly, even when quilombos prepared for them. If Tubman were surprised by one, the destruction would be staggering. Almost everyone she cared about was in Tubman. The major was there too, in as much danger as the others, thanks to her.

"Shitheads!" Tariq shouted, with uncharacteristic anger. "They're doing this on purpose."

"Of course they are," Zaria agreed. "I'd better get back and warn them."

"It will take you two hours to get back." There was fear in Nailah's voice. "Even if you make it back before it hits, they won't have time to prepare."

"I'll have to steal a stratoskip to get there on time." Her mother nodded and ordered Tariq to go with her. Tariq hugged Persis and Nailah goodbye. Her brother was a sensitive man, but she was impatient to leave, and her farewells were quick.

Chapter Twenty-One

The replica of the Taj Mahal was magnificent, despite its small size. The major had seen holograms of the long-destroyed structure, but he could not remember it in enough detail to help with the hologram puzzle he was piecing together. He had been surprised to learn that Breiche was also an aficionado of puzzles and games and could offer several options to pass the time. The two of them sat across from each other, each manipulating controls. The major was chained to the pillar, but he felt unencumbered, so intent was he on recreating the image of the architectural marvel.

"I can see it's taking shape," Masika said, his dreads bouncing as he reentered the room. He had gone out to see if he could find an unjammed comcast frequency on which to view the day's news.

"Any luck?" Keoki called from the patio.

"None." The signals had been jammed for several days now, and even Palmaran frequencies were being interfered with. Since that afternoon, there had been a complete news and communications blackout. Masika was not the only one worried about it. He and Keoki closed the sliding doors to the patio, so Breiche and the major couldn't hear their conversation.

The major hoped the jamming had to do with his kidnapping. Maybe Major Stojic and Captain Lobo knew he was in Tubman and alive. Maybe Magaly had lied when she told him he was presumed dead. They were planning a rescue mission and blacking out communications to ensure their success. He couldn't convince himself of any of it.

He turned his attention back to the puzzle, happy to have the activity. He had always found puzzles relaxing. Breiche appeared to enjoy them too. Absently, the major struck up a conversation with him. "Magaly is due soon." She would be spending the night.

Breiche consulted his chrono. "She'll be here in an hour or so." He did not seem anxious to see her.

"She seems very different from the rest of you, if you don't mind my saying so. More—I don't know—angry." The major was on the alert for differences he might exploit. Certainly, Magaly was a source of tension.

"She has her reasons," was all Breiche would say.

"Which one of you programmed the barge to collide with the refinery?"

Breiche didn't respond. The major continued, "You could have done it. You've had the training. But I can't believe you would have put so many lives at risk."

Breiche smiled, without looking at him. "So you assume it was Magaly?"

"I don't think so. She wouldn't have the technical know-how. No offense, but Palmaran technology is decades behind ours. Besides, if it were Magaly, the death toll would have been a lot higher. That leaves Zaria. She was trained on Earth. She has the expertise."

"What makes you think any of us had anything to do with it?"

He ignored the question. "But someone had to give her the access codes, a Peacekeeper, or a Consortium pilot, maybe."

"Still looking for your conspirators, Major?" Masika said, entering from the patio. Keoki stepped from behind him and slipped into the kitchen, wrinkles of amusement framing his almond eyes. The major held the Black man's gaze.

"Is it so difficult for you to believe that we Palmarans could carry out sabotage without Terran help?"

"You had help," the major maintained, but for the first time he considered the possibility that there hadn't been a traitor. Perhaps they had acquired the access codes through unwitting accomplices.

Masika waved his hands in rebuttal and went into the kitchen. The major went back to rebuilding the Taj Mahal.

The hologram suddenly blurred, and the major blinked, trying to clear his vision. Across the table, he saw Breiche shake his head slowly, his eyes shut. He glanced toward the dreamcatcher, gently swaying in its corner.

"Quake!" Breiche shouted. "Get out! Quickly!"

The rumbling started softly, but quickly grew. Clay dust rained down from the ceiling. Then the vibrations began.

Appearing suddenly at Breiche's side, Masika pulled him out of the chair and began to guide him toward the patio. But Breiche waved him angrily away. "I'm fine. Get the major out of here!"

Fine dust powdered them as Masika unlocked the chains that bound the major to the pillar. They ran out through the patio and into the courtyard. People from nearby homes were pouring into the fields. Over the din, he heard Breiche shout, "Where is Keoki?"

Masika called, "He's still in there! I'll go back for him." Struggling to keep his balance, he headed for the house.

"Be careful!" Breiche shouted after him.

The major looked around him. Houses were collapsing, people shouting and crying. Joachim, the young boy who gardened with Breiche, was running back and forth in front of a heap of rubble, tears pouring down his face. He could see the child's lips forming "Mommy!" again and again.

Breiche was looking at him. It was clear that he understood that the major meant to escape and that he could do nothing to stop him. His look spurred the major to action. He ran, half anticipating that Magaly would confront him at any moment. Drawing on his memory of the maps he had studied on Keoki's handpad, the major ran through the plazas and never once heard Breiche call out to him. But he did hear voices, many of them, shouting and crying in misery, fear, and despair. He ran past them all, determined to reach the base, easing his guilt by promising himself he would help through the Peacekeeper efforts that were surely already under way.

Chapter Twenty-Two

Landslides in the wake of the quake had torn chunks from the cliffs lining the coasts. As Zaria flew over towards Tubman, she lifted one hand off the controls to give Tariq's shoulder a quick squeeze of comfort.

Just outside the quilombo they looked down on what had been a clay-brick cottage. Once set well back from the edge of the cliff, half of it now lay in ruins. What remained perched precariously on the edge. Only moments before, Tariq had been berating himself for not having jump-started the stolen skip more quickly. Now he was silent.

As they descended, Tariq nudged her and pointed to a woman, hunched near the cottage on the barren reddish ground. Half-hoping to find other survivors, Zaria and Tariq braced for landing.

Tariq broke into a run, heading for what was left of the cottage. Zaria, medi-kit in hand, ran to the woman huddled in the red sand.

It was Jung-Min, sobbing quietly. When Zaria was close enough to hear, she called out, "Priya is still inside!"

Tariq quickened his pace toward the ruins poised to slide down the cliff.

Jung-Min was caught in a crevice, both legs broken and sticky with blood. Zaria tried to keep her face calm and her voice steady. Her small kit would be inadequate to treat compound fractures. "You're going to be fine, Jung-Min," she said, "just fine." Jung-Min only nodded, her eyes fixed on Tariq.

As Zaria cauterized the wounds and patched them with synthaflesh, she could see Tariq cautiously prodding the wreckage. He called to Priya but got no answer.

A piece of the roof broke loose and was tumbling down the cliff. Jung-Min cried out. Zaria sprang to her feet. Tariq glanced back at the two women briefly, then leaned into a small dark opening formed by two collapsed beams and pulled back, shouting, "I think she's in here!" Gingerly, he began to clear away the debris, uncovering a stone beam. Zaria could hear him grunt as he tried, unsuccessfully, to lift it. "Zaria, give me a hand here!" he called.

With Jung-Min's nod of approval, Zaria went to help her brother. Together, they attempted to lift the beam, only to send more debris tumbling down the cliff. They stopped abruptly, aware that further attempts could send the wreckage into the sea and Priya along with it. Zaria could just make out Priya lying under a pile of clay bricks, roof tiles, and chunks of stone.

"Check the skip," Tariq suggested. "Maybe there's a laser torch or something we can use to move this thing."

Zaria dashed off to the stolen skip. As she opened the cockpit hatch, she was startled to see Major Eaglefeather opening the one opposite. For a moment they stared at each other.

Through her shock, Zaria realized that something must have happened to her father to enable the Major to escape. "How did you get away?" she demanded. "Is my father all right?"

Eaglefeather was equally shocked. Nevertheless, he responded, "He's okay as far as I know. The quilombo is a bit of a mess, though. You're going to need help. Simcoe can provide it."

"Don t worry, Major, I won't stop you," Zaria said wearily. She understood that she had just caught him trying to steal the skip, but Priya was the priority. There was no time to worry about this ignorant Peacekeeper. "Go on back to Simcoe. Tell them how brilliantly successful their tactic was."

"What are you talking about?"

"They predicted this quake, ten hours ago. Maybe they knew

about it before that, but they never warned us."

She watched his face. "I find that hard to believe. If the Consortium had predicted this they would have issued a warning. That's standard procedure." His brows furrowed, he looked less assured than he sounded.

"They issued a warning within the compound, but not outside. Why do you think I came back here tonight? I wanted to warn people, but I was too late."

"I don't believe you," he insisted, but she could see the doubt in his face.

"Then check for yourself," she challenged him, "Try to use the transmitter in the skip, any frequency. See if you can contact anyone."

Zaria rapidly searched the skip, while the major stood motionless, but she could find nothing useful. "Shit!"

"What?"

Before she could answer, they heard Jung-Min scream. The wreckage was caving in on itself. "Hurry up!" Tariq called.

Zaria turned and ran back to Tariq. "No torch in the skip," she told him. "I didn't see anything that might help." Tariq was staring past her.

"Major," he said, "what are you doing here?" Zaria whirled around to find him almost at her heels.

"You need my help," he said simply. "I gather someone is trapped in there."

Tariq nodded. "We're going to have to do this the old-fashioned way. There's a stone slab over there we could use as a fulcrum. If we can move that serasteel beam, we might be able to rig up a lever."

Minutes later, as the sky grew lighter, Tariq told Zaria, "Once we lift, pull her out."

Crouched in readiness, she nodded. The men grunted as they pushed down on the beam. The stone column shifted and Zaria quickly crawled into the hole. Only that afternoon Priya had been dancing and singing, joyous at her new life with Jung-Min. Now, even in the dim light, Zaria could see their efforts had been for nothing. Priya's skull had been crushed by a stone slab.

"Come on!" she heard Tariq call to her. Small chunks of stone began to cascade down on her.

"She's dead," Zaria choked out.

The reply was a sharp crack, the lever snapping. As Zaria brushed against the opening, the debris above fell on Priya, missing her own head by centimetres. What remained of the cottage tumbled into the sea below. The three of them backed up quickly as the sand beneath their feet began to give way. From behind them, Jung-Min's wail pierced the night.

The men stood silently, watching the wind catch fragments of the cottage and hurl them to the rocks below. Zaria walked slowly to Jung-Min, who was now sobbing convulsively. Crying herself, Zaria fell to her knees, held her and gently rocked her back and forth. "They were just married today," she heard the major explain to her brother. Vaguely, she wondered how he knew that.

"The quilombo is on fire," the major said matter-of-factly. Zaria looked toward the distant valley. Crimson and orange streaked the darkened sky. Thick black smoke rose into the air.

Feeling tears staining her cheeks, she turned away from the burning quilombo. The major had gone back to the skip. Let him escape, she thought. He had helped try to save Priya. He wasn't a bad man, just on the wrong side. She turned away.

But Eaglefeather did not go. Leaving the hatch open, he returned. standing before them, eyes averted, he said, "There must be other survivors in need of help. Jung-Min is in shock. Get her in and let's see what we can do."

Chapter Twenty-Three

Young Joachim lay still and quiet now, in the arms of his mother, her head wrapped in a crude blood-stained dressing. She was not among the worst of the injured, so she sat quietly as two overwhelmed paramedics ministered to others.

A handful of able-bodied, and not so able-bodied, neighbours sifted through heaps of rubble looking for survivors. A few residents were still unaccounted for.

The newborn baby boy cradled in Jamal Breiche's arms was also still and quiet. Holding the sleeping baby made him feel less useless than he had at its birth. He could only watch helplessly as the young paramedic cursed in frustration. Though still a girl as far as Jamal was concerned, she had fought to keep the mother alive, but within minutes she'd had to focus her efforts on saving the unborn baby, for it was clear the mother would not survive.

He looked around him. Bodies ringed the field. His house, although damaged, was one of the handful that were still standing. Keoki, who had survived with a mild concussion, pronounced three of the five structurally safe, including Jamal's. Eventually the survivors would move into them, Jamal knew, and his tiles and furniture would be under assault again. He cursed himself for being a cranky old man.

A medi-skip was lifting off from the makeshift skip-strip in the centre of the field. It would ferry the more seriously injured and return with supplies. On the far side of the courtyard, Jamal saw the slow-moving figure of Tuyet Chowdhury. She spoke briefly to a woman who was awkwardly trying to bandage her hand. Letting the bandage dangle, the woman pointed to Jamal. Tuyet hurried towards him, slowing only to skirt a wide crack in the earth. When she reached him, he silently handed her the baby.

Tuyet carefully took the sleeping baby, studying its face intently. Jamal remembered examining his own newborns just that way many years ago. Lately, he had been looking forward to becoming a grandparent. Only months ago, he had been jealous of Tuyet's joy at the news that her son's partner was pregnant.

"Thank you, Jamal," Tuyet whispered. "It's amazing he can sleep through this. Is he all right?"

"He wasn't sleeping a moment ago. The paramedic is sure there's no damage to his lungs."

Under other circumstances, Tuyet would have given a proud grandmotherly smile. She nodded. "Is there any hope my son will be found alive?"

They turned toward the wreckage that had once been the home of Tuyet Chowdhury's son and his partner. Sixto Masika was among those digging in the rubble, looking for survivors. They would be digging for some time. The scene spoke for itself. Tuyet nodded again. Drawing the baby close, she walked toward the rubble to watch the digging.

Jamal lurched over to landing strip. The medi-skip was due back soon. Surely there was something he could do to help.

He was helping to unload medical equipment and supplies when he overheard the pilot tell the young paramedic that the quilombo's hospital could handle no more casualties. The skip would be flying out empty. The young paramedic began to argue with the pilot. The rains were scheduled to begin in an hour, and, dammit, they couldn't just leave people out in the open. Jamal could see she was exhausted. "Let him go," he said. "We can move those who can be moved to my house and to the others that are still standing."

The moving of the injured had just gotten under way when Jamal spotted Magaly, with Huseni and Rahim in tow. She looked dazed as she stopped to take in the ruins. Then she reddened in anger and rushed at Sixto. She and Jamal reached his side at the same time.

"Where's the major?" Magaly said. Sixto exchanged a quick look with Jamal. "He'd better be dead," she warned, as Sixto hesitated.

"He escaped," Jamal calmly told her, "but he's on foot. He won't get far."

"He'd better not or we're all up the Cygnus gravity well without a thruster. He'll be heading back to the base. Rahim, you take a groundskip through the pass. Huseni, fly a skip up around Goree. I'll take the underside of the cliff."

"If you have access to a skip, I think there are better uses for it," Sixto said. "Communications are down. Supplies and medical personnel need transport. The Tubman hospital is full. The injured are going to have to be taken for care outside of the quilombo ..."

"I understand that. But our lives are at stake if Major Eaglefeather makes it back to Simcoe." Her expression remained unchanged. Sixto and Jamal watched her soberly. "I'll be back as soon as I can."

Sixto set his jaw and blinked. "Don't kill him. Otherwise you're no better than they are."

"Not to mention you would have murder charges hanging over your head," Jamal added pointedly. "Imhotep extradites people for that, you know."

An incoming stratoskip drowned out her response. The skip did not bear the medi-serv emblem. They waited for it to land. Jamal was relieved to see his two children climb out. The major followed. Tariq called for a stretcher for Jung-Min. When it became apparent that they were the full complement of the stratoskip's passenger manifest, Jamal knew that Priya Said was dead.

Sixto bolted for Jamal's daughter The two clung to each other as paramedics took over the care of Jung-Min. Jamal hugged his son, feeling Tariq's tension drain. The major waited by the skip.

Magaly walked up to the major. The others fell silent. "Why did you come back? You could have been halfway to the base by now."

"He could have been all the way there, if he'd taken our skip," Zaria said. "He had the chance and didn't."

Tariq agreed. "He helped us with Jung-Min and others we found injured on the way back."

"Your arm's bleeding again," Jamal said. "You should have one of the paramedics take a look."

"They're busy. I'll be all right," the major said softly.

A low rumbling began, followed by familiar vibrations. A child screamed, setting off a chain of cries and shouts.

"It's only a tremor!" Jamal called out. "Keep calm, everyone." He staggered off into the courtyard, imploring people not to panic.

The aftershock subsided and with it the clamour in the courtyard. Jamal went on directing the moving of the injured into the houses. Sixto, with Huseni and Rahim, returned to the ruins. As Zaria looked for something useful to do, Magaly cursed angrily.

"Damn! Our communications are still jammed, so we can't contact Imhotep to find out if we should expect more aftershocks."

"That can be fixed." The major had said little since he decided to help them and nothing on the way to Tubman, just gazed silently out the windscreen as they flew over the devastation. Zaria had been too preoccupied with the crisis to wonder what he might be thinking.

"The jamming is designed to break up the signal into particles so that no one can make sense of it."

"So we've noticed," said Magaly.

"But it's not randomized. The base would have figured you wouldn't be able to reprogram your comnet to compensate, so it didn't bother. Your receivers can be set to reassemble the jumbled signal into something intelligible. I can do it for you."

"Will you?" Zaria asked. The major was offering to commit treason.

He nodded without enthusiasm. "Take me to a receiver."

"Right this way," said Tariq. The two men climbed back into the stratoskip. With Tariq piloting, they lifted off.

"What's gotten into him?" Magaly asked Zaria.

"He's becoming disillusioned, I think. He was shocked to find out that the Peacekeepers had deliberately jammed our comnet, so we wouldn't have time to prepare for the quake."

"Sure," Magaly snorted. "Didn't he give the order to jam us in the first place? Days ago?"

"I don't think he did," Zaria said tightly and walked away to help her father.

Chapter Twenty-Four

The comnet was finally online, the image blurred. Evidently, the major had been successful in re-programming the quilombo's receivers. In the only room of Jamal's house not crammed with the injured, Zaria tapped at the console, fine-tuning the reception. Her father had just joined her. It was the first break they'd taken since the quake hit fourteen hours earlier.

The comcasts said there were twenty-six known dead in Tubman, with seventy people still missing. Fires were now under control. The imager panned across the ruins. Relief efforts were receiving official support from Imhotep. The nearest quilombos had sent medi-skips to treat and fly out the injured. Militia contingents would be arriving to set up temporary shelters for those left homeless. The base and compound, it was reported, had experienced little damage and only minor casualties.

The Palmaran Governing Council had called an emergency debate on its response to what was believed to have been the Peacekeeper jamming of the comnet. The Peacekeepers denied responsibility for what their spokesperson called "communication interference" and cited natural causes as the likely cause. They offered to help in the relief efforts. Nevertheless, demonstrations had broken out in quilombos across the planet, with protesters calling for everything from reparations to independence to war.

Then came a hurried interview with Sixto Masika, Professor of Geology, Tubman University. Zaria leaned forward in her chair.

The comcaster Summarized Sixto's comments. Professor Masika was disappointed that people were talking in terms of vengeance, she said. Then the comcast switched to a clip of his interview.

"The quake," he explained, "was caused by the wide-scale mining of our moons. The moons are losing mass and their orbits are shifting, and with them the gravitational forces. The volcanic eruptions, the tsunamis, the quakes we've had for the last two decades are the result. And it will get worse. The Consortium and the Peacekeepers have to go. Pressuring them into better relations with us is irrelevant. The mining has got to stop."

The clip stopped. His views, said the comcaster, were controversial and not widely accepted by experts. "Although," she conceded, "more and more Palmarans are calling for Terran withdrawal. This is Imelda Hranov reporting from Tubman Quilombo."

Zaria muted the audio and looked at Jamal exasperatedly. "Well, it took her about two seconds to discredit everything he said."

"If you think the comcast's bad, forget checking out Peacecom," he told her.

A tired-looking young man in a paramedic jumpsuit appeared at the doorway. "Elder Jamal, there you are. I've just spoken to the hospital. No beds are available and they don't expect to have any available any time soon. We'll have to spend the night here."

"Don't worry," Jamal assured him. He welcomed the change from the suspicion and distrust he usually met as a Terran and former Peacekeeper. The paramedic nodded his thanks. "Oh, by the way, that Peacekeeper is downstairs asking for you." His contempt for the major was clear in his tone. Too tired to take issue with him, Jamal and Zaria went down to greet the major

After re-programming the quilombo's main receivers, the major had left with Tariq to join a search party looking for survivors at the badly damaged bibliotek, the region's major reference centre. No one had talked to him about his change of heart. He had wanted to help with relief efforts and that had been taken at face value. Earlier, Jamal had offered him a place to sleep for the night, and he had returned. He stood just outside the cottage, exhausted and alone, his black uniform caked in red mud, chestnut stubble shading his jaw,

Jamal led him through the room that had earlier served as his cell. Three quake victims lay on cots, their accusing stares tracking the major's self-conscious movements. A dozen others, propped on cushions on the floor, glowered at the major. Jamal said firmly, "Major! Looks like you've been on a dig. The comnet's working fine. We just turned off the comcast."

The major shook his head slowly. "Guess you've given up on your furniture."

Jamal paused in confusion. "You were worried my blood would stain it," the major said with a tight smile. Jamal, now beset by questions coming from the room of injured about the comcast, had no time to answer the major. How many were dead? they wanted to know. How many injured? How many homeless? What was the damage? What was being done about relief? What was the government going to do? What about the Consortium? Was there news of this one's partner, that one's son?

Zaria took the major by the arm and led him to the patio, away from the voices. She pressed the button on the wall and the door slid shut behind them. "Imhotep has declared us a disaster area," she said. "They're sending in relief supplies and workers. And they want an official apology from the Peacekeepers, who still deny they jammed us."

"They're lying."

"We know that," she said. "Everyone does. But there isn't much we can do about it."

She wondered if he would be willing to tell the public what he knew of the jamming, but before she could ask, she saw someone walking into the courtyard.

A young blond man wearing a paramedic jumpsuit stepped up to them. Hanif Bjorndahl. "Well, well," she mumbled, ignoring the major's perplexed look, "just in time."

Bjorndahl's face wore a look of determination. "Hello, Zaria," he said briskly, intending to forge past them.

"Hanif" Zaria blocked his path. "Glad to see no harm has come to you. Can the hospital spare you?"

"The hospital sent me."

"Good. I guess things are calming down a bit."

"Somewhat," he said, trying unsuccessfully to get past.

"This is Major Leith Eaglefeather of the Peacekeepers," Zaria said, waving her hand in the major's direction.

Bjorndahl did not look at the major "Excuse me," he said to Zaria.

"Hanif," she pleaded, her green eyes fixed on his. "Please."

"He won't believe me."

The major watched, frowning.

"What have you got to lose?" she asked.

"Bjorndahl? Corporal Hanif Bjorndahl?" The major interrupted, his face alight with recognition. "I read about you. You're listed as missing in action."

"Is that so?" Bjorndahl asked, bristling.

"Yes." The major felt too tired to make an issue of Bjorndahl's desertion.

"Tell him, Hanif. He's got to know."

Bjorndahl sighed. "I worked with Major Reynolds, your predecessor. I did not agree with many of her, uh, methods."

"Such as?"

"Her interrogation techniques." Bjorndahl glanced at Zaria, who nodded for him to go on.

"Yes? Go on," the major urged.

"She used torture to get information and confessions."

"I assume by that you mean she mistreated prisoners. Did you report her?"

Bjorndahl sighed again. "No, sir I mean, no, sir that's not what I meant. When I said torture, I meant torture."

"All the more reason to report her to Major Stojic or the colonel, if what you say is true."

"The colonel knew, sir" In the face of the major's presumption of authority, Bjorndahl had suddenly become submissive.

Peacekeeper training ran deep.

The major hesitated before his next question, “Just what are we talking about here?”

With a nod, Zaria prompted Bjorndahl. “Tell him, Hanif.”

“She set up a special interrogation room, in the docking section, Compartment Two. She put in a neuro-link, operated from a control console in an adjacent room. The link stimulates the brain’s pain centres. The victim feels intense pain, but there’s no tissue damage, nothing shows.”

The major kept his voice level. “I’ve heard that some Palmarans claim that the base has such a device, but I didn’t believe them and I don’t believe you.”

“I assure you. Major it exists. It has been used. Many times.”

“On whom?”

“People Major Reynolds considered terrorists. Those who lived through it were shipped to prison camps on the asteroid belt near Jupiter.”

“So you have no proof.”

Zaria spoke up. “A year ago, we liberated two Kituhwa comrades en route to a prisoner transport headed off-planet. In their debriefing, they told us the had been tortured with the device. Even we doubted their story, thinking they were suffering from some kind of post-traumatic disorder. You see, the technique leaves no physical scars behind. The symptoms of stress are not significantly different from those of any former prisoner. We were prepared to dismiss the matter, when Corporal Bjorndahl walked into the quilombo.”

Bjorndahl continued, “I couldn’t stand it any more. I saw a woman being tortured to death. I had warned them. She was old, had a weak heart. They wanted to know about her daughter The death certificate read natural causes. I left that day.”

“You didn’t report this to anyone?”

“Like I said, the colonel knew.”

“You could have gone over his head.”

Bjorndahl shook his head and turned to Zaria. “I told you he wouldn’t believe me.”

"Major," Zaria insisted, "this goes well beyond Colonel Welch and the Peacekeepers at Simcoe. Only the Peacekeepers' high command on Earth could have developed such a device. And that would have required secret funding. My guess is that the Terran government contracted with the Consortium to build and test it here on Palmares."

"That's a big jump," the major said. "I can believe that the Consortium is corrupt and that the Peacekeepers stationed here are their willing accomplices. But you're suggesting a Terran conspiracy. When I get back to the base, I'll certainly look into his charges about Major Reynolds. But as for the Terran government ..." He turned to Bjorndahl. "Come back with me, Corporal. I can help you cut a deal, get the charges against you dropped if you agree to testify against Colonel Welch."

Bjorndahl stepped back and shook his head vehemently. "I'm not going back, Major. Never. My life is here now." Then he quickly stepped inside Jamal's house.

Zaria's look made the major uncomfortable. "I might not be able to do much about this if he won't agree to come back with me."

Her hands slapped her sides in exasperation. "What does it take. Major? What does it take?"

His face flushed with anger, he squinted in the sunlight. "What do you want me to do?"

She frowned. "Your ancestors were indigenous North Americans. You must have read your history."

"My history?" he said, puzzled by the sudden change of topic.

"Do you remember anything about the struggles against the Europeans?"

"What's that got to do with this?"

"As people after people encountered the Europeans, they debated what to do. Whether to respond peacefully or violently. Whether to cooperate or resist. Whether to be assimilated, or not. Some peoples cooperated. Some resisted peacefully, others not so peacefully. Some withdrew to other territory, even as the land shrank before them till there was nowhere to go. Different people had different responses. And not one worked. They were decimated. In some cases, entire civilizations disappeared."

"Your point being?"

She regarded him soberly. "There are only fifteen million people on this planet, Major. Whether we fight openly or not, we don't stand a chance against Terran Peacekeepers."

"You think it will come to that?"

"It has."

"If you're right, then whatever I do will make no difference to the outcome of your struggle."

"That could be true. But some of us don't feel as if we have a choice. We take a stand, because we have to."

"Did you save my life in the hope I would join you?"

"That was Sixto's hope."

"But you gave the order that kept me alive. Why?"

She wasn't sure herself what the answer was. "I don't know. I just — I couldn't let them kill you." She turned away.

"Ho, there!" called Sixto, from the distance. He sprinted toward them, a cloth sack bouncing over one shoulder. Bounding onto the patio, he kissed Zaria's lips with a smack.

Zaria turned back to look at the major, her arms folded across her chest. Glancing from one to the other, Sixto stepped back from Zaria. "Seems I interrupted something." The major said nothing.

"We just talked to Hanif," Zaria explained. "Our major here is, shall we say, skeptical."

"I see," Sixto said.

She wondered if he really did. "I have work to do. See you later," she said to Sixto and went inside.

Chapter Twenty-Five

The major's shoulders sank as the door closed on Zaria. Masika stayed behind, shifting his weight from one foot to the other. He cleared his throat and asked, "Major, will you walk with me?"

"Why?" the major grunted. "Isn't there more we can do here?"

Sixto picked up the sack. "We've got a lot of hungry people to feed. I thought I'd pay a visit to the community garden."

With a look back at the shut door, the major said, "Yeah, sure." He was too tired to think clearly.

As they walked through the greenhouse, Sixto reached out and picked fruits and berries, tossing them into the sack he had slung over his shoulder The major found he no longer saw Masika as his enemy. A part of him admired Masika as a man of principle, a man fighting for what he believed in, though what he believed was, of course, preposterous.

A stratoskip, bearing Peacekeeper markings, passed overhead. It was the second in as many hours, delivering much-needed supplies and food to the quilombo. Not enough to make amends for what has been done here, the major thought.

As he followed Masika through the garden, he went over what lay ahead of him when he returned to the base. First, he would look into Bjorndahl's allegations. Under the circumstances, it might be better to contain his fury over the jamming of Palmaran communications prior to the quake, at least for a while. Once he determined whether the neuro-link existed, he would decide what to do next, but he would have to be careful. Only Colonel Welch could have issued the jamming orders, and there was no telling what he might do if he were crossed.

They talked little and only of things of no consequence as they climbed the path leading to Merae Goree. At the top, Masika steered the major away from the clearing and led him into thick brush. The steps off the path and into the brush rekindled memories of his capture. Only hours earlier he had believed the Kituhwa were going to kill him. Now, in the aftermath of disaster, he found himself puzzled by the camaraderie he felt for Masika and the others.

Why had they come? The fruits here were aesthetic, not edible. Why had Masika led him here? He was uneasy, though nothing in Masika's manner suggested danger, just subterfuge. I need sleep, he reminded himself. I need to clear my head and think.

"Why are we here?" he asked Masika. By now, the density of the brush put them in near darkness. Saying nothing, Masika led him to an upright stone slab in a dim clearing. The major saw it was a large grave marker.

"Do you know why we call this place Goree?"

"Goree was an island off the cost of Senegal where captured Africans were held before being shipped to the New World as slaves," the major responded. He assumed that he had not answered the question as Masika had hoped, but at least he had known something of the meaning of the place.

"It was," Masika said, "a place of unimaginable brutality and suffering. The slave trade lasted for four hundred years, you know. Goree was the last people would see of their homeland. After the end of slavery and on through the centuries, many Africans in the diaspora travelled there. Even now, some of them — some of us — go to the site. I did, many years ago. It was amazing. I thought I could hear the crack of the whip, the crying of mothers and children. I cried myself, right then and there, on the tour."

"Is this also a place of suffering? Or did you simply wish to honour your ancestors?" The major moved closer, to read the words carved on the stone. He didn't recognise the language, but below the inscription the writing was in a local derivative of Spanish. A list followed. He didn't understand everything, but he did recognize a name: Tranquilino Masika.

"My father," Masika confirmed, watching him. "He died here, twenty-seven years ago. He and the others on that list are buried here. My father was a geologist, like me. He and his colleagues were meeting with a group of Terran journalists, over there in the clearing. They were going to present proof that the increase in volcanic activity is linked to the Consortium's mining operations on our moons.

"About halfway through the conference a stratoskip, flying several kilometres off of its flight plan, crashed into the side of the cliff. The pilot bailed out, but the cargo — ethramine gas — went down with the skip."

"Ethramine gas?" The words sounded vaguely familiar

"Used in the processing of quilidon. It's lethal to humans. They were all rendered unconscious and died in a matter of minutes. The gas had dissipated by the time their bodies were discovered, but the autopsies confirmed the cause of death."

The major glanced at the date on the stone. "You were a child at the time." His own father had died when the major was in his early twenties. It had been painful but nothing to compare with what the eight-year-old Masika must have felt.

"Even the journalists died," Masika went on. "And that is what I want you to remember when you leave us."

"Why?"

"Because it was the first in a series of events that convinced other journalists to leave Palmares. They questioned the official account of the accident and they got a message in return: nothing that jeopardized the mining operation would be tolerated. They began to have accidents, some of them fatal, till more and more of them, fearing for their safety, left. The ones who stayed behave themselves."

"There are several journalists in the compound," the major countered, doubting he had the strength to get into another political argument. “We find them a pain in the ass. You should consider yourselves lucky they don’t harass you like they do us.”

“Yes, those that remain produce a rather skewed version of events for the Terran public. But few ever come out here to the quilombos to check on the truth of a story. Few ask us what’s really going on. And when they do, we’re given a few seconds to respond or rebut. Information sent to Earth is tightly controlled.”

The major had heard it all before, but everyone, even the Peacekeepers, complained about the media. “Palmarans are sometimes interviewed.”

“Only when they say what they’re supposed to. Or when there’s someone standing by to discredit what they say.”

He asked what he hoped would get Masika to make his point. “Who do you think is behind this. And why?”

“I know this is going to sound crazy,” Masika answered without hesitation, “but the Terran government is a shell. Palmares is just the first stage in a New Galactic Order. Earth’s resources are exhausted. Its survival depends on its being able to keep on subordinating all the colonies in the galaxy, each with its specific role: Mars and the asteroid belt for strategic minerals, Basilea for thyanite, Palmares for quilidon ...”

“Look, Masika, you people have convinced me that the mining should stop until more studies are done. I can even accept that the Consortium and Peacekeepers acted criminally in not announcing the quake. I’m prepared to investigate Bjorndahl’s allegations of human rights violations. But I really can’t accept that this is a Terran plot to dominate the galaxy.”

“I understand,” Masika said. “It’s hard to accept. Many Palmarans don’t believe it. There are times when I, myself, hope I’m suffering from orbital dementia, because if what I think is true, I don’t know what to do about it.”

The major didn’t doubt that the Palmarans were being victimized. That Masika and his colleagues should react as they did was not surprising. If he could be among the first Terrans to show good faith, perhaps mutual suspicion would subside. “Things will change, Masika. When I go back, I’ll see to it.”

"Don't do anything stupid, Major. As far as they're concerned, you're expendable. Count on it. If you start asking questions, they're going to snuff you out quicker than a blow torch in a vacuum."

"I can take care of myself. I have contacts in the Peacekeepers on Earth. If Colonel Welch is behind this, he will be disciplined."

"You've come a long way, Major," Masika said, frowning. "But not far enough."

"I won't defect. If that's what you expect, you'd better kill me now."

"Major, I wouldn't have gone to all the trouble of saving you if I wanted you dead. No, if we're going to lose, I want to go out with dignity. I won't dishonour myself by becoming the very thing I oppose."

"I can see why you get on Magaly's nerves," the major said. "What more do you want?"

Masika reached into the folds of his clothes and pulled out a small datacube. "Here. Take this."

"What is it?"

"Proof that Palmares is breaking up. The results of twenty-five years of research. The finest minds on Palmares contributed to it. I assembled it myself."

"Why are you giving it to me?"

"Because you're a credible source."

"You want me to pass it along to some of my journalist contacts here?"

"No," Masika said emphatically. "No journalists here. The cube has a list of sympathetic Terran journalists. The list is old, but even if you can get the information to only a few of them, I know they'll use it."

"You're putting a lot of faith in journalists on Earth."

"Not at all. Our strategy is two-pronged, Major. First, to make it too expensive and dangerous for the Consortium to remain here. That is why we carry out sabotage."

"And the second prong?"

"To let Terrans know what's happening here, force them to ask embarrassing questions. Maybe they'll be outraged enough to pressure your government to leave us be. More realistically, we hope we can force the Consortium to exhaust its resources in covering up its activities. Besides, we suspect that it's doing what it does here wherever it operates. Maybe we have allies out there."

"And you expect me to help you?"

Head high, shoulders straight, Masika looked at him. "I'll leave it with you, Major. You do what you think best."

The major hesitated, then nodded and pocketed the data-cube. He was confused, but he was not going to do or say anything that might discourage Masika from letting him leave. "Are you letting me go? Now?"

"Letting you go? You know as well as I do that you could have left long ago. You stayed of your own free will, at least since the quake. The question is; are you ready to leave us now?"

"No," the major replied, surprising himself. "No, I'm not. I need an answer, just one more before I go. Did you get the ignition codes to sabotage that barge from an informant?"

"I don't believe it! After all that's happened, you're still worried about that."

"I need to know. You don't have to give me a name. I just need to know."

"And would you believe me? I don't think so. If I were to tell you there was no informant, you'd say that I was protecting someone. If I were to tell you there was, you'd say I wanted you to waste your time trying to find out who it was."

"I don't think you understand what I want to know."

"Don't I? Then what is it exactly ... Ah! I get it! You're trying to find out if Zaria was involved."

"She and her father are the most likely suspects. They trained as Peacekeepers."

"Would you love her any less if she were responsible?" Masika asked.

"Love her?"

"It's all right, Major. I'm not worried about it. And you shouldn't be either"

"I don't have any — I don't know what my feelings are for her." He had no idea why he was confiding in this man.

"I'm not surprised, after everything she's put you through. There's no harm in telling you the truth. You have no proof, after all. If it will help you trust me, it's worth it. Zaria played a prominent role in that operation, but I hope you remember that no lives were lost."

"Pure luck!"

"No, not luck at all. As a matter of fact, I suggest you think back on all Kituhwa operations. There have been no casualties, except when the Peacekeepers engaged us. And on those occasions, more of us Kituhwa died than Peacekeepers."

"Well, thanks for your honesty. Can I ask how you acquired the helm control codes?"

"A blissfully sleeping Consortium pilot who frequents the Aristide."

"I see." It was plausible.

Masika handed him the sack of fruit and berries he had picked. "It should take you about six hours to reach the compound on foot." He offered the major his hand to shake — an unusual gesture for a Palmaran. "Good luck, Major. If you have the integrity I think you do, you're in for a rough time."

Chapter Twenty-Six

Zaria and Magaly half dragged themselves into Sixto's house. They were W^^not surprised to find no sign of him. They had exhausted themselves aiding the relief efforts and had lost track of how many hours had passed since they'd agreed to meet here.

The situation was finally under control. The missing had been accounted for. Makeshift shelters were being erected for those who had been left homeless. Food and water rations were being handed out. Medi-workers from across Palmares had flown to Tubman, urging those locals who were still standing to get some sleep. Architects and engineers would arrive in the morning with construction droids and begin rebuilding Tubman. The debate on who to blame for the disaster raged on.

The morsel of food on Zaria's fork felt as heavy as a lead weight, but her belly growled in anticipation. From the other end of the table, Magaly, her eyes framed by dark circles of weariness, pushed her plate away.

"I'm too tired to eat." She rested her head on her arms.

"I'll never be that tired," Zaria said, shoving the fork in her mouth.

"I wonder how Jung-Min is?"

Zaria paused in her chewing and squeezed her eyes shut. She felt Magaly's hands gently taking one of her own.

"I think I know how you feel," Magaly whispered. "Like nothing will ever be the same again."

"I feel guilty. Because no one in my family was harmed."

"That's what it feels like," Magaly agreed. "I don't think you ever get over it. I never have."

"You mean your parents?"

Magaly nodded. In all the years they had been friends, Magaly had never talked about her parents' deaths, and Zaria had never asked. She had wondered if Magaly had any memory of them at all, given that she had been only six when they died. "Do you want to talk about it?" Zaria asked cautiously.

Letting go of her hand, Magaly leaned back in her chair and stared at the ceiling. After a moment she spoke. "I don't remember them any more."

"That's not surprising. You were very young when they died."

"No," Magaly said, "but I was very young the last time I saw them." She lifted her head and looked Zaria in the eye. "They didn't die until last year, actually." Zaria tried not to look surprised.

"They were arrested. Suspects in a bombing. I was little. I didn't understand everything, and no one explained anything to me. I remember the Peacekeepers. It seemed like there were hundreds of them. They burst into the house. I was terrified. They seemed so big. They beat my dad brutally. Ripped me from my mother's arms while she tried to fight them off. They took me away and brought me to a woman's house. I cried all night. The next day they brought me here, to Tubman, and told me I had a new family. Just like that."

"Unbelievable." Zaria murmured.

"But it happened. My new parents had no idea what had happened to me. They had been told that my real parents died in a flood. They had no reason to believe otherwise. They were good people and after a while I came to like them. I never knew what had become of my parents until last year, when my mother died. A prison guard with a guilty conscience sent me her personal effects. There wasn't much, but there was a journal. It explained everything, starting with their arrest."

Magaly paused and swallowed hard. "They were tried and convicted of twelve charges, including murder. The life sentence they got wasn't much of a surprise. Over the years, they agonized over what had happened to me. Almost every journal entry contained some speculation about me: what I looked like, where I lived, was I safe. They died with their questions unanswered. My dad on Phobos, my mom on Io." Zaria could only shake her head.

"I never told anyone. I was never sure what would happen if I did." Magaly's eyes moistened. Zaria stood, walked over and wrapped her arms around her friend.

"How can things like that happen? No matter what they might be guilty of, prisoners still have the right to communicate with their loved ones."

Magaly lifted her tear-stained face from the crook of Zaria's arm. "I think your precious Sixto would disagree. He considers the taking of another human life unforgivable."

At last Zaria understood the root of the friction between Sixto and Magaly Looking into her friend's face, she said, "If that's what Sixto believes, he's wrong."

"I know that you love him. I've tried to accept it. It shouldn't matter to us anyway, but..."

"It matters."

"Just don't have children. Not now, in the middle of all this. It wouldn't be fair"

"No," Zaria agreed, "it wouldn't."

They held each other for some time.

Finally sleepy, they retired to the bedroom, stripped down to their underwear and fell asleep beside each other on Sixto's bed.

The holo-imager hovering outside the window turned and flew off. Satisfied with what he saw, Captain Lobo briefed his troops.

Chapter Twenty-Seven

Someone had helped themselves to a meal. From the trail of clothes leading to the bedroom, Sixto judged that it was Magaly and Zaria. He decided not to disturb them, but Magaly, ever alert, walked briskly into the main room. She did not look as tired as she should have. Still running on adrenaline, Sixto supposed.

They hugged briefly. Though tired, Sixto was eager for news from other parts of the quilombo. They exchanged notes on who had died, who was injured, what buildings were left standing. He'd had this conversation with everyone he'd run in to in the hours following the quake.

Magaly suddenly cut him short. "What finally happened to our major?"

Sixto steeled himself for an argument. "Gone back to Simcoe."

She had guessed as much. "Why would he go back? After all he's seen here?"

"I don't really know," Sixto confessed. "He's probably confused, but I think he'll come around. Eventually."

"What makes you so sure?"

"I gave him the data-cube."

"You gave him the data-cube?" she repeated, her voice rising. "The datacube?"

"Yes. What's the problem? It's not as if there aren't several copies."

Her movements abrupt, Magaly quickly collected her clothes

and got dressed.

A droid rolled in with a tray of food. "Want any tea?" Sixto asked Magaly, while pouring his own.

"You just handed over a list of our journalist contacts on Earth to the chief of security, along with the identities of the Kituhwa's best scientists. And you ask me if I want some tea? That's it, Sixto. The end. I'm leaving the Kituhwa."

"That's up to you," Sixto wearily told her. He was not about to defend his actions or try to talk her out of it. Either way would be futile. "Where will you go? What are you going to do?"

"I'm going to fight," Magaly replied, equally resigned to the uselessness of debate. "They're going to get what they give. For every Palmaran life a Terran will die. That's the only thing they understand."

"You can't win."

"Then I'll go down fighting. Unlike you, I'm not going to wait around and see if they develop a conscience. And I'm not waiting for Major Eaglefeather to come around. That day might never come."

Sixto finished chewing a mouthful of food. "All you'll do is push a peaceful resolution even farther out of reach."

"The Terrans have already done that."

"I assume Huseni will join you. Maybe Rahim." They had always backed her in the past.

"Their choice."

Setting his mug on the table, he looked at her. He had no doubt that the Peacekeepers could easily crush armed resistance and no doubt that Magaly knew it too. Her announcement meant she was ready to give her life.

"I'm sorry things have come to this," Sixto told her sincerely. "You and I have provided some balance to the Kituhwa. Our differences have made it simple to find the middle ground. You are the Yang to my Yin."

She sneered. "Perhaps I always will be."

It was not until she had gone that Sixto noticed Zaria standing in the doorway of the bedroom. He could see from her face that she had heard everything. She walked slowly to him and they hugged.

Zaria stepped back. “Don’t worry about Magaly, Sixto. I’ll talk to her”

“She sounds determined.” Sixto didn’t look at her. “Perhaps it’s for the best.”

“I don’t think so,” she said sharply. “It’s bad enough we split from the Menchista. We’re a small group. If we split ourselves any further, we risk becoming ineffective. Besides, I’ll miss her.”

“I’ll never understand that,” he admitted, shaking his head. “Do you agree with her? Do you think it was a mistake to give the major the data-cube?”

“You did the right thing. He’s a good man. He may need some time, but I think he’ll help us.”

Sixto reached out and pulled her close again. Maybe he should give it all up, move away, marry Zaria and start a family. Get out before it was too late, before the Magalys on both sides started a full-scale war. Looking into Zaria’s face, he was tempted. He could do nothing to change what was to come. Was he so important that his staying would make the difference between war and peace? He didn’t think so.

He kissed her “Marry me,” he whispered into her ear

Zaria pulled back slightly and studied his face. “Of course I will.” She hugged him close again.

o

The blast jarred them apart. “Down on the floor!” a voice commanded. A dozen Peacekeepers launched themselves through the smouldering doorway.

“Face down!”

“Do it, now!” shouted another. “Or you’re dead!”

Sixto pulled at Zaria’s sleeve, signalling that they should obey. A brownskinned woman with freckles pointed her weapon at Zaria’s face. “I said down!”

They dropped to the floor

"Hands above your heads," someone ordered. "Spread-eagled."

As they were patted down, Sixto protested, "What do you want? You have no right to come in here, destroy my home, intimidate me with —"

"Shut up." A Peacekeeper jumped across what was left of the threshold. Captain Lobo—Sixto recognized him from comcasts—swaggered over to the couple. His eyes lingered on Zaria longer than was necessary or respectful. She was still wearing only panties and one of Sixto's T-shirts.

"They're clean," the freckle-faced woman reported.

"On your feet," the captain commanded.

"You'd better have a warrant and a mediator with you or this breach of Palmaran sovereignty will make the quake a ten-second news item —"

"I said shut up." He raised an arm to strike Sixto. Zaria blocked the blow. Around them, the troopers tensed, but no one fired. He grabbed Zaria's hair and yanked her off balance. "And I thought you were just one of his whores. I guess you prefer female bodyguards, Masika?"

To Sixto's relief, Zaria chose not to defend herself. She glared at the captain with such defiance that he faltered for a moment. Proud that no fear had crossed Zaria's face, Sixto stepped forward. "Let her go. It's me you want."

"Yes." Lobo jerked Zaria's hair again before releasing her. "It is you I want. You're under arrest for sabotaging the refinery." He turned to his troops. "Take him!".

"No!" Zaria said as two troopers moved in. "You have no right to be here. You have no mediator. You have no warrant, and you couldn't get one if you tried. Sixto had nothing to do with it!"

"Zaria! Be quiet and let me handle this," Sixto implored.

"They'll kill you!"

Lobo turned on Zaria. "And how do you know he had nothing to do with sabotaging the refinery?"

"Because — I know him. He wouldn't do something like that!"

"Then who would? You, perhaps?"

"No," Sixto interrupted. "She had nothing to do with it."

Captain Lobo turned to one of his men. "Take him." Half a dozen Peacekeepers escorted Sixto out the door. Sixto looked back at Zaria, small and vulnerable in a sea of black uniforms.

Chin held high, shoulders squared, back straight, she mouthed, "I love you" as his guards took him into the night.

Lobo turned his attention to Zaria. "Your name?"

"Zaria Aquene. Can I go now?" She was anxious to report Sixto's arrest to Imhotep and to Magaly, who might act on the information more promptly and effectively than the Governing Council would.

The captain ordered a black-suited women to check her handpad for a database entry under Zaria's name and other Peacekeepers to search Masika's house. That done, he turned back to Zaria. "You look familiar. You were at the crash site when we went to investigate."

"She's a dancer" said one of the uniformed men. "At the Aristide. I've seen her there."

"Right. The dancer at the Aristide. That's where I've seen you before." Lobo looked thoughtful. "Ah, yes. The Aristide. That place has a lot of potential. A lot of potential as an intelligence gathering operation, don't you think, Ms. Aquene?"

"That's ridiculous, as any court of extradition would agree."

"Yes, you're right," he admitted, "that's why we're not going to extradite you." He barked at his troops again. "Take her too!"

"What's the charge?" a woman in uniform asked bravely.

"She's a suspect being held for questioning. When we finish here, our next stop will be the Aristide."

Chapter Twenty-Eight

The intern was puzzled by Major Eaglefeather's wound. The major claimed to have injured his arm in a stratoskip crash, yet the scar under the synthaflesh suggested a laser burn, and there were no signs of the head injury that he claimed had left him wandering in a stupor for days. But, she told herself, these security types were always getting injuries that didn't match their stories, just accept what you see, treat it and keep your mouth shut, she had been advised. The wisdom of that advice was underscored when Colonel Welch walked in. As he and Major Eaglefeather greeted each other, the intern made a quiet exit. There were some things she had no interest in knowing. The major went through his story again. He had been injured when his skip crashed. He had only a hazy memory of wandering, of being treated briefly by a Palmaran he ran into, then being pointed in the direction of Simcoe and walking in a daze until he arrived at the compound gate. He had no idea how long he had been away. His only clear memory was of the last few hours, walking home.

"A lot has happened while you were away, Major," the colonel told him.

"I'll have Major Stojic fill me in." The major longed for sleep.

"Yes, well. Major Stojic is one of the things that happened while you were away."

"Oh? How so?" the major asked, pulling on what was left of his uniform.

"Your theory that a traitor helped Masika has been confirmed.

It was Major Stojic. Apparently, Masika was giving him a steady supply of bliss, in exchange for confidential information."

The major had not expected that. "How do you know this is true?"

"We got a full confession out of Major Stojic."

"A confession? He confessed to being Masika's accomplice?

"Your young Captain Lobo is a fine interrogator. Perhaps being deprived of bliss helped convince Major Stojic to talk."

"A man suffering from withdrawal is hardly a credible source, Colonel. Does what he says check out?"

"Captain Lobo is working on that," the colonel said, just a little too quickly. "We picked up Masika a little while ago. He's being questioned now."

The major fingered the data-cube in his pocket. "I'd like to talk to Major Stojic."

"That won't be possible. Major Stojic is dead."

"What happened?"

"He was an old man, dependent on bliss. When he was cut off... I'm sorry. I know you two were — well, I'm aware you socialized occasionally. It came as a shock to all of us."

The colonel patted the major's shoulder "Get some sleep. Captain Lobo has everything under control for now. You can take over the investigation after you get some rest." Without waiting for a reply, the colonel left.

*

Shinichi led the group of twelve men and women to the Aristide at dusk. There was no way Nailah and Persis could mistake their intent, but the two stood toe to toe with Shinichi and barred his way.

Shinichi could not look at Nailah. True, Nailah had a reputation for collaborating with the Peacekeepers. True, she had married a Terran. But in his personal dealings with her, Shinichi had always found her to be an honest and compassionate woman.

The group behind him, however, had no reservations. Angered by reports of Tubman's devastation and by Peacekeeper complicity in it, their mutters turned into shouts at the two women blocking their way into the club.

"Get out," Shinichi told Nailah. He regretted that he had to sound more threatening than protective, and for a moment, he thought they were going to have to knock her down to get inside, but Nailah only turned to look at Persis. Shinichi wondered what Nailah would have done had the younger woman not been present. Nailah put her arm around Persis' shoulders and led her out of the Aristide.

With the women gone, the group broke from behind Shinichi and through the door. He found little satisfaction in watching their work. After a while, when the Aristide was beyond repair, he left them to it and went home.

Chapter Twenty-Nine

The major's hope that the information on Masika's data-cube would tell him what to do next was not fulfilled. The cube spat out reams of diagrams, formulas and simulations. The geology and the physics equations on the console screen were beyond his comprehension, but the names of the researchers meant the Kituhwa could stand behind the data. In frustration, he pulled the data-cube from its slot and fingered it.

Suppose it were a forgery? What did Masika have to gain by giving it to him? There was no explanation. At best, fact or forgery, the cube might buy some time while scientists debated. Time for what? To make the Peacekeepers suspect the journalists? That made no sense. And what if Masika were right? What if he held the proof that Terran mining would destroy Palmares? Proof covered up by Terran scientists? If it was fact, Masika was risking the safety of dozens of people, scientists and journalists alike. And if I transmit it to Earth, the major said under his breath, I can kiss my career goodbye.

Captain Lobo was entering the outer office. The major shoved the cube into his pocket.

"I sent for you two hours ago. Where have you been?"

"Interrogation Room Two. I was busy, Major. Welcome back."

"Busy at what?"

"Interrogating our newest prisoner, Sixto Masika. Surely you've heard."

"I heard. I was reviewing your report. It's incomplete."

"I can finish it now, if you like." Captain Lobo seated himself calmly, unfazed by the major's apparent anger. Clearly, he assumed the colonel would approve his actions. Maybe he's right, thought Eaglefeather.

"You didn't have Imhotep's permission to launch a police action on Palmaran territory. Consequently, you had no extradition order, which means you launched an unauthorized mission, in violation of the Quetzal Treaty, and kidnapped a Palmaran citizen."

"I have a terrorist in custody. That should count for something."

"Not with me, it doesn't!"

Captain Lobo looked at his chronometer, as though bored. "You and Colonel Welch seem to have a difference of opinion on that, Major. The colonel congratulated me, suggested I could be up for promotion. Maybe you two should sort out your differences before we talk."

He stood up, ready to leave, but paused when the vidphone sounded. The major punched a key in response.

Corporal Pham's image appeared. "Captain Lobo — uh. Major Eaglefeather," she stammered. Clearly, she had expected the captain to answer her call. The data scrolling across the screen's base showed that she was vidphoning from the medical centre. "It's Masika. He had a stroke or something. We found him in his cell. They've pronounced him dead."

"What!" the major shouted. "A stroke? Sixto Masika was thirty-five years old. How long was he unconscious? Who saw him last?"

"He was brought from the interrogation room about an hour ago. Captain Lobo was in charge of the questioning. I only just came on duty, Major, so I don't know what Masika's condition was when he was returned to his cell. All I know is that when the droid delivered his meal, he couldn't be roused." Corporal Pham's look implored him to accept her version of events.

"Corporal, I'll be down to the cell block shortly. In the meantime, I want you to get back there. Seal off the area and look for evidence."

"Evidence of what?"

"For the time being, just act on the assumption that we have a suspicious death. Treat it accordingly."

"Yes, sir," she replied, gathering composure with her new responsibilities.

As he disconnected, he turned to the captain. "I assume Masika's interrogation was recorded."

"It was. It's on a cube, but it won't help you. He didn't say much."

"What did you ask him?"

"What you would expect. How he did what we know he was responsible for. The names of his accomplices. The usual."

"And your methods?"

"I'm offended that you ask me that, Major" The Captain did not look in the least discomfited. "I did nothing illegal. No drugs. No probes. Since he never consented to the truth detector we couldn't use it. I think we should consider suicide as a possibility."

"Suicide?"

"Unfortunately, he had time and opportunity to take a delayed-action poison. It's not unheard of for fanatics to kill themselves to avoid going to trial."

"Exactly what evidence did you have against Masika?"

"Excuse me, Major?" Captain Lobo seemed baffled by the question.

"Evidence, Captain. Why he was arrested."

As if the matter were of little consequence, he replied, "Stojic's confession."

"I see. Is that on a cube too?"

"Of course, Major" His tone was cooperative, but his eyes were cold.

The vidphone tone interrupted again. "Major Eaglefeather," the colonel cautiously greeted him. "I thought I told you to get some rest."

"Colonel, I've just been informed that Sixto Masika has died in our custody. Cause of death ..."

"Stroke. Yes, I heard. Is Captain Lobo there?"

The major stepped aside so the vidphone could focus on Captain Lobo.

"In my office. Captain Lobo. Immediately. And bring the holo-cubes of Masika's interrogation."

"Yes, sir"

"Colonel," the major broke in, "I haven't seen those cubes yet. Masika's death falls under my jurisdiction."

"Yes," agreed Welch, "and I'm sure you'll do a bang-up job of it when your head is cleared by a good night's rest, Major. Captain, report to my office. Now."

The colonel disconnected. With a smirk, the captain rose from his seat. "Perhaps we can finish this in the morning, Major"

The major said nothing as he watched him go. He sat for several minutes, reviewing courses of action. Mechanically, he tapped at the keys that would call forth the record of Major Stojic's arrest, interrogation and death. He could not gain access. He had typed in his security code without a second thought. The screen read: UNAUTHORIZED SECURITY CODE. ACCESS DENIED.

He should have remembered. Only Major Stojic, Colonel Welch and he himself had access to secured files. The colonel would have ordered the codes changed the night the Kituhwa faked the crash on Merae Goree.

Though he knew it would be pointless, he tried to open the file on Masika. The results were the same. He'd have to get the new codes before the files were deleted and the evidence lost forever

The vidphone broke his concentration. "We've got some trouble inside the compound. Major" It was Corporal Riwi Odilon, speaking into the vid-link on his wrist. Voices in the background made it difficult to hear clearly, but Eaglefeather recognized the scene behind Odilon. The corporal was standing on the beach below the Aristide.

"The Aristide was just burned down by rioters," Corporal Odilon continued. "It was already ablaze when we got here. The firefighters have been working at putting it out for over an hour, but there won't be much left of the place. Not worth our time to search."

"Search?"

"We did manage to pick up two of the people on the list Captain Lobo gave us. A Nailah Aquene and a Persis Nguyen. We'll bring them in right away."

"No," the major commanded, "stay on the site. I'll be right there."

"Aye, sir," a confused Corporal Odilon replied, with a salute.

Chapter Thirty

Captain Lobo watched Colonel Welch insert the cube in the imager. It was the only record of Masika's torture and the captain's complicity in it, and he rather favoured its destruction. The colonel, however, had other plans.

Masika was dead and they had nothing to show for it. The stubborn man had died before telling them anything of value. The colonel hadn't bothered to hide his annoyance at Captain Lobo's bungling, but at least they still had the woman.

"Major Reynolds never gave me much of an opportunity to learn about the inducer," the captain tried to explain. "And of course there were no records ..."

"Captain, no more excuses." The colonel crossed to the credenza where he kept the liquor and poured himself a pale green liquid. The office was already littered with dirty glasses, emptied hours ago during the celebration of Masika's arrest. "At least there was no obvious tissue damage."

"Were you able to put a stop to the autopsy, Colonel?"

"Yes. I'll leave it to you to clean up the lab results and find someone to sign the certificate. It would look suspicious to say he died of a stroke at his age. Make it look like a suicide by poison. Is that understood?"

"I'll do my best."

"Your best had better exceed your performance thus far Captain. Have you had a chance to question the woman?"

The captain's mouth was dry from fear that he had made

another mistake. "No, sir, I haven't had the chance yet."

"Then you haven't seen her medical scan results, I gather"

"No, sir Not yet."

"Well, take a look."

Captain Lobo called up the file from the colonel's console. "What the hell!" he sputtered as he scrolled down the screen.

"Indeed," the colonel said. "There's no question. The DNA scan proves that the embryo is Masika's."

The captain smiled. All was not lost. "She probably knows as much about the Kituhwa as he did. Maybe even more."

Gulping the last of his drink, the colonel strode back to the imager "All right, let's take a look at what we have here."

*

Nailah and Persis looked fragile, sitting together on the beach. The four Peacekeepers, two women and two men, including Corporal Odilon, kept a respectful distance, but their presence was intimidating as they stood and whispered to each other

The blaze on the cliff above was still smouldering when the major arrived. He thought the two women looked dazed and tired, but their expressions turned expectant at the sight of him.

Corporal Odilon saluted smartly. "Major, I'm sorry about the guy on the list. We combed the area but we couldn't find this Tariq character ..."

"It's all right, Corporal. These people are only wanted for questioning. I can take it from here."

Odilon hesitated. "Are you sure, sir?"

"Absolutely, Corporal. You and your people are dismissed. Good work."

"Well, if you say so, Major. Thank you, sir"

After rounding up his troops, the bewildered Corporal departed.

The major knelt beside the women. "Thank you, Major," Nailah said, gracious as ever. "You make a habit of showing up at just the right time."

"Not in time to save the Aristide. I'm sorry. Do you know who's responsible?"

Persis shook her head, but Nailah contradicted her "Yes, and I can't blame them. They thought we were collaborators."

"Have you come from Tubman?" Persis asked anxiously. "Do you have any news of Tariq or Zaria?"

"Or Jamal?" Nailah added.

"They survived the quake," he said vaguely. "Nailah, I need your help." Time was short and he had to be direct. "It's imperative I get a message to Magaly. I can give you clearance to leave the compound to deliver it. Will you?"

"Yes," she said immediately.

Chapter Thirty-One

Still clad only in a T-shirt and panties, Zaria turned heads as two female Peacekeepers walked her through the subterranean corridors. She had been given a routine scan, but no one had questioned her. When the last of several doors in the underground maze slid open, she was shoved into her cell. The thick metal door slid shut with a thump.

Trying to convince herself that she might find a way to escape, Zaria examined her cell. A lumpy cot, a water-stained sink and a sweaty toilet were all it held. The light was dim, coming from a source in the high ceiling. There was a sour, cleaning-fluid stench. She sat on the cot and shut her eyes. Soon I'll be grateful at the sight of this cell, grateful for a break in ...

She pressed her fingers to her temples, as though she could squeeze out her fear. This was not a dream. She was in a Peacekeeper prison cell, waiting to be interrogated. Maybe she'd be lucky. Maybe Imhotep had found she was being held. Maybe someone was already trying to get her out of here. She wanted to hope but knew the chances were slim. She thought about Sixto and tried to steel herself against what awaited them. Don't dwell on it, she told herself, forcing herself to think about what in the cell she could use to escape. No ideas came to her. She didn't know if she would be brave.

When they came for her hours later, she hoped it meant a respite for Sixto. They didn't answer when she asked where they were taking her.

The office they led her to was large and well-appointed, conveying the power of its occupant. The two men in it, Colonel Welch and Captain Lobo, sat and appraised her then told her to sit in a large neo-leather armchair. The upholstery was cold and clammy against her skin, causing her nipples to harden under her T-shirt. Captain Lobo's eyes went from her breasts to her legs and back but avoided her face. His staring made her nauseous.

The guards were told to wait outside the door. She could smell alcohol and saw half-filled glasses on the hardwood console and credenza. Sixto's capture had been cause for celebration.

"Good morning, Zaria Aquene Breiche," said the colonel, consulting the screen at his console. "Dancer and musician. Graduate of the Peacekeepers' Institute. Retired as a lieutenant, junior grade." He looked over at her. "Found in a state of undress in the company of one of the most notorious terrorists in the galaxy." Zaria kept her eyes and her breathing steady.

"Let's get on with it, shall we? Are you Masika's lover or bodyguard? Or both?" She looked at him but said nothing.

The captain took his turn. "Or maybe he was just a figurehead. Maybe you're behind the sabotage. You've got the training. You could have made the necessary contacts when you were a Peacekeeper. You'd know who you could persuade or trick to give you the Consortium's codes."

He got up and walked over to her "And the Aristide was the perfect base of operation, wasn't it? Between the Bliss and the liquor and the stupor-inducing entertainment, the secrets slipped out. Right into your ears." By the time he had finished, his pink face was almost touching hers. She blinked, unable to focus, and turned her face away.

The colonel spoke. "No one knows you're here, you know. I could kill you both, make it look accidental and leave your bodies where they won't be discovered for a hundred years."

She closed her eyes to shut them out. Fear is normal, she repeated to herself. They want you to feel so frightened you'll cooperate with them. When she opened her eyes again they were smiling at her "On the other hand," the colonel continued, "I can inflict such pain on you that you'll beg to die. You'll do anything to make it stop and be grateful for the chance to live out the rest of your pathetic life mining Jupiter's asteroid belt."

"Or we can get it over with now," the captain suggested. "Cooperate with us and save Masika's life." Zaria flinched at the mention of Sixto's name.

Encouraged, he went on. "Tell us everything you know about the Kituhwa, and I'll spare your friend." Abruptly, he switched on the imager. Sixto writhed on the floor of a bright white room. The soft hum in the background could not block out his gasps and moans.

The hum suddenly stopped and the room's light softened. In a heap on the floor Sixto breathed in short heavy gasps. His body twitched. The humming began again and he jerked violently. He cried out, but his words were unintelligible.

"You want us to stop, don't you?" the captain said. "Well, we can and we will, on one condition. Tell us everything you know about the Kituhwa. That's all you have to do, and we'll leave him alone."

The hum stopped for a moment, then started again. Tears welled in her eyes, and she began to tremble from helplessness. When the hum stopped again, she could hear Sixto sobbing softly. They were breaking him. "Please," she said, struggling not to cry. "Please stop."

She looked away as the hum began again, eliciting a pitiful scream from Sixto. She felt small and powerless in the big black chair. She breathed deeply, then said, "No more. I'll say whatever you want. I sabotaged the refinery. Not Sixto. He's innocent. Leave him alone." Having successfully fought back tears, she faced the colonel. She was no longer frightened.

The captain switched off the imager "All right," the colonel announced. "That will do for a start."

A buzz from outer office interrupted them. The colonel slammed his hand on the intercom button. "What is it?" he barked.

A nervous voice responded, "Major Eaglefeather is on his way to see you. Colonel. He says it's urgent. A security matter."

The colonel turned to Captain Lobo. "See to her and be careful — I don't want her to end up like Masika."

Chapter Thirty-Two

From the reception area where he waited, the major watched two female guards enter the colonel's office, but he was too preoccupied to think about what their presence might mean. When they emerged, with Zaria between them, he thought his legs would buckle beneath him. Her eyes met his and then she was gone.

They had failed to tell him that Zaria had been arrested with Sixto Masika. She was a dancer at a local club, hardly significant. Masika had told them nothing, according to Captain Lobo. If that were true, the only hope they had of gaining information on the Kituhwa rested with her.

Captain Lobo came out of the colonel's office. The major kept his face impassive. He was not about to reveal himself to the captain or the colonel. The captain, however, avoided his gaze and hurried away.

Of course, thought the major, the colonel has reprimanded him for causing Masika's death, and now he has to make good, with Zaria. There was little time to lose.

"Major," the colonel greeted him, "you don't look as though you took my advice about getting a good night's rest."

"I was busy, Colonel. An informant brought me some disturbing news. About the Kituhwa." Pausing for effect, the major was glad he looked dishevelled. His appearance would lend credibility.

"In the aftermath of the quake, the Kituhwa has been recruiting. Amassed an armed band. They're heading for the compound."

"Would they be so stupid as to attack us?"

"Apparently. But my informant was able to give me a fairly detailed account of their plans."

"Excellent, Major," the colonel congratulated him. "Go on."

"They're going to create diversions inside the compound — looting, arson, that sort of thing. While our people are running around, they'll hit the reactor."

"The reactor! They're crazy. They could turn Palmares into space dust."

"I'm aware of that, sir. I'll need your permission to deploy troops along the southwestern wall. That's where they'll enter."

"Of course,Major. Take whatever precautions you need."

"But I'll need more people than I have assigned to me. I'm going to need everyone from datakeepers to skip mechanics at my beck and call. I need to convince the Kituhwa their plan is working, that we've been distracted. The only way I can do that is by having our people running helter-skelter over the compound responding to one crisis after another."

"I understand," the colonel authorized with a nod, "do it."

"I'll need the new security codes, Colonel."

"New codes? Oh yes, of course." He quickly scribbled the series of numbers, letters and symbols and handed them to the major.

"We're superior Colonel. We have the numbers and the technology. They don't stand a chance."

"Make sure they don't."

o

It had been difficult for Magaly to understand the message that Nailah had passed on. She didn't want to believe it, but Sixto Masika was dead.

The memory of their last conversation haunted her. She had chosen armed resistance. She had accepted the ultimate risk. So why, in the name of justice, did Sixto have to die? But guilt and grief would have to wait. Zaria had been at Sixto's house at the time of his arrest, and no one had seen her since. Likely, she was being held somewhere on the base. Magaly would have to move quickly.

Kituhwa piled into stratoskips warming in the lavender dusk. Magaly looked round at Huseni, Keoki, Rahim and Persis. Their faces looked far too solemn for their years as they silently squeezed themselves and their equipment into the passenger section behind Tariq, who sat in the pilot seat.

Losing Sixto and Zaria was to lose the heart of the Kituhwa. Sixto had been more than their comrade; he had been their moral leader, their visionary. Zaria had been the calm, rational strategist who put his ideas into practice.

The engines started, and Magaly caught a glimpse of Nailah pressing Jamal Breiche's hand to her heart. They stood there as the skip lifted off and veered with the others toward Simcoe.

The ease with which Breiche had organized them into teams with specific assignments had not surprised Magaly. He had fought a war. He had also strongly cautioned them to avoid taking lives. It was advice she had no intention of heeding.

o

The first explosions ripped through the compound at sunset, just as the major had requested. No doubt Magaly was enjoying herself tonight, he mused, relieved that his message was being acted on. He shouted orders to the crew of support personnel assigned to him. Looking awkward in Peacekeeper battle fatigues, datakeepers and skip mechanics fanned out in groups of six to eight. The major could only hope that their inexperience with the weapons they had been issued would not result in serious injury or death. He had ordered them to set their weapons to stun, but they had no training and he had no choice. Crack Peacekeepers were on a fool's errand at the far reaches of the compound where, with any luck, they would remain until he could get Zaria out.

He left Corporal Pham at the master console in the operations room outside his office. She basked in the responsibility of coordinating the movements of the teams. On the pretext of preparing for the main event, an attack on the reactor, he went to his office.

The security codes were not necessary for his first act. The comlink transmitted the contents of Masika's data-cube to the subspace addresses of every Terran journalist in its database. Once that was done, the data-cube would be erased.

With the transmission on its way, the major punched in the new code and gained access to the base's security channel. He began with the security net he had recently installed and shut it down. By the time he had finished, all but one of the base's security measures had been deactivated. He left the security for the detention section below online.

A quick glance through the glass at Corporal Pham in the outer office assured the major he had not aroused suspicion. As she nodded reassuringly to him to show that all was well, he tapped the keys required to call up prisoner files, then balled his fists in frustration at finding that Major Stojic's and Masika's files had been deleted. Whatever information they had once held could now incriminate no one. He had no time to lament. He called up Zaria's file intending to delete its contents as well. However a phrase in the last entry caught his eye: "embryonic tissue of eight day's gestation ..."

His hands were shaky when he tapped the keys to delete the file. The news did not really change his plans, but it did disturb him. Wasting no more time, he checked the power cells on his handweapon. It was fully charged. Returning it to its holster, he left his office and told Pham he would now be joining the troops stationed near the reactor There was a wistful look in her eyes as she wished him luck and bade him goodbye.

Chapter Thirty-Three

Feigning panic in her ruse as innocent-citizen-pursued-by-angry-mob, Magaly easily gained access to the base's reception area, and was surprised to find only a single harried young woman on duty behind the massive security console. The woman's momentary indecision over how to help a refuge-seeking resident gave Magaly the opportunity to stun her. She fell with a dull thud.

Magaly stepped over the unconscious woman. Her weapon still drawn, she scanned the screens and lights on the security desk. Before she had time to read a word, the entire console winked out. Furiously, she flicked switches and slammed keys, hoping to restore the link. She had no way to call up the base's floor plan. The controls were dead. She wondered if it were her comrades or the major who had managed to shut the power down. Perhaps he knew that Zaria had been arrested with Sixto and had his own plans to rescue her, but Magaly couldn't count it. She had to get to Zaria.

As she set her weapon on kill, she thought back on what rescued Menchista detainees had told her about the layout of the base. Then she picked a corridor at random and set out to find the detention cells she knew were somewhere below.

Compartment Two looked exactly like the other interrogation centres, a cold metallic room, colourless and unfurnished. It was easy to spot Zaria, curled up on the floor. She lay with her arms pressed against her ears, her hands clasped tightly behind her neck, her face hidden. She was soaked with sweat, and the glistening streaks on the cell floor around her testified to the writhing she'd done earlier.

At the observation port, the major forced himself to look away from Zaria and at Captain Lobo. The major had walked in unannounced. The captain had uttered a startled "Major sir!" while getting to his feet.

A guard, one of the captain's men, pushed a button on the control panel. The low hum stopped. The major tried to recall the man's name and could not. He did, however recall the loutish, fiftysomething face. The memory of a previous encounter, in which the guard had made clear his contempt for Palmares and all things Palmaran, told the major that the guard would probably stay loyal to the captain.

The major stepped into the observation room. "Well, Captain," he said, "has she talked yet?"

"No. We haven't actually begun to question her."

"Then what are you doing?"

"Major," the guard cut in. "I been doing this for years. Trust me. Give them twenty minutes under the beam first. Then ask questions. You'd be surprised how cooperative they are."

The major jerked his head in the direction of the guard. "Was he on duty when you held Masika here, Captain?"

"The pulse has been decreased by half. She won't be hurt." Zaria had not moved. The major scowled. "She'd better not be, but that's not why I'm here. She can wait. We have bigger problems right now. The Kituhwa are planning on attacking the reactor —"

"I know. I just spoke with Colonel Welch on the vidphone. He said you were in charge."

"That's correct. And I need you. Captain, out there with the rest of the troops. I want you to take command. I don't want a single Kituhwa to get through."

Captain Lobo saluted. "Yes, sir."

"According to my informant, we have no more than fifteen

minutes." He handed the captain a data-cube. "You can study my plan on the way."

The captain saluted again, though his expression suggested he wanted to question the order, and left.

Alone with the guard, the major ordered, "Get her out of there and back to her cell."

The guard turned his back and pressed a button. As the locks to the interrogation room's door clicked open, the major drew his weapon and fired. The guard fell to the floor

The major pushed the thick doors apart. When Zaria saw him, she tried to push herself to her feet, but her arms were trembling so that she could not. Regretting he could not be more gentle with her, he grabbed her under the arms and pulled her upright. Her eyes glazed over and she groaned as she began to sink to the floor again.

"No, you don't," he said, tugging at her. "We don't have time for that. We've got to get you out of here."

"My hero." She tried to laugh but could not. "What took you so long?"

"I was doing my nails." He pulled her toward the door

"What about Sixto?"

"He's gone." At least it wasn't a lie. "Come on. I've got a skip waiting."

She seemed to take him at his word and made an effort to walk.

Chapter Thirty-Four

His face illuminated only by the flickering light from the burning communications tower, Tariq told Persis they were done. He pressed a button on the communicator strapped to his wrist. "Tariq to Huseni. Do you read me?"

"I read you!" The voice that crackled through was jubilant. "I take it your mission was successful."

"Yes. And yours?"

"I'm watching a beautiful sight," Huseni told him. "Half the skips and shuttles are ablaze."

"Only half?"

"Well, the Peacekeepers are going to need the rest to evacuate."

Huseni's cockiness made Persis smile. The fires within the compound walls were few and carefully chosen, the fuel storage depot, the skip-strip and the communications tower being the principle targets of their raid.

The tower was last, according to plan. True, jamming the signals made it harder for the Kituhwa to contact each other, but Jamal wanted to keep the troops guarding the reactor out of touch with what was going on in the compound until the very end. Most of the Peacekeepers they'd run into were not trained for combat, as the major's message had promised. They had been easily stunned or overpowered.

At last the tower was destroyed and jamming ceased. Communications in the region went back online. Soon word of the raid would reach the seasoned troops stationed at the reactor awaiting an attack that would never come. Tariq and Persis wasted no time in getting to the rendezvous point. As the skip's engine warmed in the middle of a quiet plaza, they waited with Huseni's team for Magaly. Persis tried to hail her on her wrist communicator

None of them had agreed when Magaly insisted that she would head out alone, but there had been no time to argue. Persis had watched her go, confident that if any of them could survive without backup, it would be Magaly. Now it seemed her confidence had been misplaced.

They had kept trying to contact her, none willing to suggest leaving without her. When Persis saw black-suited figures flitting in and out of the buildings around the square, she knew they had waited too long.

Tariq lifted the stratoskip into the air. Bolts of brightly-coloured energy bolts whizzed toward them, as the Peacekeepers below attempted to shoot them out of the sky. Tariq fed the engines more power. If its engines were hit, the skip would explode.

The blasts consumed layer after layer of the energy shield. At this rate, they would lose shields before they were out of range. Recognizing the choice she had to make, Persis concentrated the remaining shield energy around their engines, exposing the cockpit. It was a calculated risk. She lost.

A searing blast breached the passenger compartment.

Keoki yelped as a beam pierced his hip. Rahim was struck immediately after in his left shoulder blade.

When he heard Persis cry out beside him, it took every ounce of Tariq's concentration to remain focused on the controls. They were almost out of range. It was only when he saw the skip's shadow pass over the ruins of the compound wall that he was able to spare Persis a glance.

She was leaning back in the seat, pale, her eyes closed. Her right breast was soaked in blood. Her breathing was shallow, but she was still alive. Fighting the urge to put his arms around her, Tariq returned his full attention to piloting the skip, and made for Tubman's medical centre.

Chapter Thirty-Five

The stone tiles felt painfully cold under Zaria's bare feet. Their progress was slow, and she knew she should try to walk faster. Sixto would be in the passenger seat of a stratoskip, waiting impatiently for them. She didn't want to be responsible for the failure of the rescue attempt. "Go ahead without me," she said. "Point me in the right direction. If I can make it, I will."

Only hours ago she had been cowering in her cell. She had been tortured. She hadn't talked, but now she knew that if she spent enough time in Compartment Two, they would break her. No doubt about it. They would have to kill her. She would never go back there.

The point was moot for the moment. The major refused to abandon her. She didn't have the strength to argue; it took all her concentration to put one foot before the other. It was frustrating, embarrassing, but the major seemed to understand and kept her on her feet. There was no sign of anyone in the vast corridor that lay ahead of them.

"Where is everyone?"

"Sssh. just a little farther..."

A maintenance droid rounded the corner in front of them and rolled past. As its mechanical purr faded, she heard the footsteps that had been masked by the sound of the droid. The major spun around so fast, it made her dizzy. She fell against him as he drew his handweapon. As he reached out to steady her his weapon clattered to the tiled floor. They watched Colonel Welch and

Captain Lobo advance, their weapons drawn and levelled.

The major had wrapped his arms around her. Now, he drew her closer and half-turned, to shield her body with his own. She wanted to reject his protection and meet their adversaries head on. She pushed him away.

"The power outages gave you away," the captain said. "I didn't want to meet the Kituhwa with just a handweapon. Once I got out of the detention section, I tried to get into the weapons storage area, but the locking mechanism was dead. I figured you were up to something."

"I trusted you," the colonel spat. "You're Terran! How could you betray your own kind? Do you want Palmarans — this rabble — to take over the mines?"

She tried to focus. Did the major have help? Maybe they could overpower the two men. She was weak, but the colonel was old. If she could draw them close enough ...

The colonel paid no attention to her. "This is treason," he said. "You'll be court-martialled, Major. If you're lucky, you'll end up doing life in the asteroid belt."

"Or we could just shoot you, right here and now," the captain suggested.

"I have the information you want," Zaria whispered, edging out of the major's reach.

"What?" demanded the colonel.

Even more softly, she said, "I can name names. Peacekeepers. Traitors." The men moved a few steps closer, but they were still well out of reach.

"I want to make a deal," she offered.

"You're in no position to make deals, Ms. Aquene."

Beyond them, a shadow grew larger. Struggling to keep on her feet, she tried to make out the figure. Magaly moved towards them without a sound. The small woman had her handweapon levelled at the two Peacekeepers.

"I'll tell you anything you want if you promise to let us go."

Whether it was something in her expression, Leith's body language or Lobo's intuition that gave it away, Zaria never knew.

The captain furrowed his brows and started a pivot that he never completed.

Magaly fired decisively. The captain, hit in his torso, collapsed.

A shocked Colonel Welch spun around. Magaly fired again, but targetry had never been her strength. She missed.

As Zaria and Leith dived to the floor for Leith's weapon, Welch returned fire on the small, armed woman. His shot found its target. Hit full force in the chest, Magaly was knocked off her feet. Welch reeled around again and was taking aim at Leith when Zaria's finger found the trigger mechanism on the Major's weapon. The first shot missed, but distracted Welch from Leith. Before the Colonel could take aim at Zaria on the corridor floor she fired again.

Welch was hit. He fell to the floor, stunned.

Zaria dropped the weapon and stumbled to her fallen friend. Blood trickled from Magaly's mouth and her eyes had rolled back under half-closed lids.

Fighting tears, Zaria stroked her friend's face and closed her eyes. The major rose and stood beside her "I'm sorry. I don't know how she got here or why she came. It wasn't part of the plan." Drawing in a deep breath, he collected himself. "We're running out of time. We've got to get out of here."

She heard him, but the words didn't register. Magaly looked so small and fragile in death. Barely aware of what she was doing, she wrenched Magaly's weapon from her hand. She checked it. It was set to kill. Still on her knees she pivoted towards the unconscious Colonel Welch and aimed the weapon.

It would be so easy, she thought. No one could argue it wasn't justice. He deserves to die.

Before she could press the trigger, the major's hand came down over hers. He gently pushed the weapon toward the floor.

She shivered. The major opened his mouth as if to say something, but before he could speak she dropped the weapon, stood up and fell into step behind him. She followed him out a side door. There was no alarm. They encountered no one as they walked to a skip in the base lot.

The door opened once the major had keyed its combination into the access panel. Zaria bent to climb in, but when she saw the skip was empty, she froze.

"Where's Sixto?"

For the first time since she'd met him, the major looked frightened. His jaw moved slightly before he spoke.

"I'm sorry, Zaria."

"Oh no!" she whispered. The tears she'd been holding back since Magaly died rolled freely down her cheeks.

The major waited awkwardly. After a moment, he drew her to him and held her as she sobbed.

She climbed into the skip. With the major at the controls, they lifted off and headed for Tubman. Choking back sobs, she watched without seeing the fires raging below. Columns of black smoke towered above the skip. People swarmed over the compound. Finally, mustering some interest, she asked, "What's going on down there?"

"A diversion. Magaly arranged it." He looked down at the chaos in the compound. "Apparently, she took my request seriously. I asked for a few harmless explosions. It looks like an inferno down there."

She smiled faintly. "So you and Magaly joined forces in the end, did you?"

"Something like that." She listened as he explained why he needed the diversion. By now, the transmission would have reached Earth.

"What made you do it?"

"The realization that you had been telling me the truth all along."

She looked down as they passed over the cliff where the Aristide should have been. Numbly, she saw the rubble that remained. Steeled for more bad news, she asked what had happened.

"Everyone's all right," he assured her "An angry mob broke in and burned down the place. But your mother and Persis got out unharmed. They're safe."

Zaria leaned back against her seat. She waited for several minutes, then asked, "Did he die in that interrogation room?"

He hoped she was strong enough to hear the truth. "Yes," he finally said. "He never told them a thing."

She closed her eyes and regretted that she had not killed the colonel. The tears fell again.

With his right arm, the major reached over and gave her a squeeze. She appreciated the gesture, but nothing would ease the pain.

"There's something you should know," he said hesitantly, after she had stopped crying. Wondering how much more she could take, she said nothing.

"You're pregnant."

She did not know what to feel. Palmares was in chaos. Her family's livelihood lay in ashes. Sixto was dead. She stroked her belly. It felt no different.

"How do you know? Are you sure?"

"According to the medical scan, you're eight days along."

The sun's first light streaked over the ocean. "Nine days now." He smiled encouragingly at her.

"It'll be all right."

No, it won't. It'll never be all right. She was tempted to contradict him out loud, but held her tongue. His career was finished. He could not return to Earth. And he was pathetically in love with a woman carrying another man's child.

Two hours after their departure from the base, he set the stratoskip down in a landing lot. They elicited little interest as they walked to Jamal's house. By now, the quilombo's residents were used to seeing walking wounded. Exhausted, Zaria leaned against the major.

In spite of her fear for Tariq and her other comrades, Zaria wanted sleep. She dozed while Jamal debriefed the major on the diversions and the sabotage.

She awoke to see her mother and father weeping in each other's arms. The major stood nearby, his hands clasped behind him, looking awkward. "Tariq's at the hospital," the major said. "He's fine. Persis is wounded, but it's not serious. It's going to be all right."

All right, Zaria repeated in her head. That silly phrase again. But she nodded gratefully and slept some more.

Epilogue

The Kituhwa affair topped the comcasts for weeks. Many Palmarans regarded the Kituhwa as heroes who had forced the Consortium and the Terran government to the negotiating table. Others were frightened that a secret society could wield such power, and warned that it did not bode well for the future. Still others worried about anticipated reprisals, as rumours circulated that the Terrans were dispatching a war fleet to safeguard the Consortium's mining operations and punish those who had sabotaged them.

In any event, Zaria Aquene was tired of the attention. In weaker moments, she lamented the loss of the anonymity she'd had as a spy at the Aristide.

Studying herself in the mirror she caressed her swollen belly. Nine months had passed quickly. Soon the baby would be needing all her time and attention.

Wearily, she wished for a long vacation. So much had happened since Sixto's death. Jamal and Nailah had decided to rebuild the Aristide and were busy each day supervising its reconstruction. Persis and Tariq had married and were expecting their first child. Zaria had faced Major Eaglefeather regularly over the negotiating table for the last six months.

The information on Sixto's data-cube had reached most of the Terran journalists on the list. That and news of Peacekeeper activities on Palmares had brought down the Terran government in last month's elections, and brought Palmares its independence.

Colonel Welch recovered from the temporary coma brought on by Zaria's handweapon blast. He was hastily court-martialled and hustled off to Earth. The early comcasts had speculated that he was a convenient scapegoat, that the crimes committed against the Palmaran people had been sanctioned at the highest level. The stories faded after a while.

The Consortium had agreed to pay the Palmaran people reparations, in return for immunity. Eager to put the matter to rest, the Terran Secretary General had agreed to negotiate a new mining treaty with independent Palmares.

The major, whom the media had turned into a celebrity while journalists scrambled to verify the information on Masika's data-cube, had been appointed the chief Terran negotiator. Outnumbered two-to-one in trilateral talks, the Consortium had made painful concessions. Among these was the issuing of a majority stake in the operation to the Palmaran government. The Consortium still stood to make large profits, though not as large as it had made before. Its new contract stipulated that all mined quilidon be replaced with other appropriate and less strategic minerals. That demand had been Sixto's idea, a note in his records that Zaria had found while sorting through his work. It was an expensive undertaking for the Consoritium, but the value of quilidon more than made up for it.

With the negotiations completed and the treaty signed in last night's formal ceremony, Zaria found the solitude of Sixto's cottage most agreeable. She would raise her baby here, surrounded by memories of Sixto.

Settling herself into a chair she turned on the imager. As she had done many times over last several months, she viewed Sixto's childhood, his lectures, social occasions. It was less painful now. Her greatest worry was that she might forget him, not in the larger sense, of course, but the details: the playfulness of his eyes, the corners of his smiling mouth, the soothing feel of his caress, all that she hoped someday to describe to the child growing inside her.

At the beep of the door buzzer, she turned the imager off.

Having grown used to frequent interruptions during the months of negotiations, when rumours and idle gossip had the potential to provide one side or another with an advantage in the next round of talks, she responded promptly.

She was surprised to see the major standing in the doorway. He had never come here before. They had talked in his office, in her office, at receptions, at cocktail parties but never at Sixto's cottage.

"May I come in?" Assuming it was an official visit, she stepped aside.

He accepted her offer of tea, and while the domestic droid prepared it, they talked.

"You haven't changed anything," he said, looking around.

Remembering that he had seen this room only once, on a holo-cube, she nodded. "I will soon. I don't have anything for the baby yet."

"Right. How are you feeling, anyway?" It was the first time he had mentioned her pregnancy since he broke the news to her.

"I love this feeling of taking up space. But, except for being bigger I don't feel different at all."

He laughed. "I'm sure you will soon."

She smiled.

"Is it a boy or a girl?"

"Girl."

"Have a name picked out?"

"Magaly."

"Magaly. In some ways I understand. But would Sixto?"

"I don't know. They were my two best friends. They never agreed on anything, but they would have had they had more time. The baby will have his genes and her name."

The droid rolled in, and they lifted their teacups from its tray.

"You did an excellent job on the Palmaran negotiating team," he told her.

"I was terrible. I was argumentative, stubborn and inflammatory."

"Right. You made me look good."

She laughed.

"So, what happens now?" he asked.

"There's so much to be done that I don't know where to start. You know what they say. The real revolution begins when the fighting stops."

He nodded. "Yes. With the Palmaran government as the majority owner of the mining operations, it could become the new exploiter."

"Indeed. It's happened before." She sipped more tea. "By the way. In all this time I've never thanked you for—uh—"

"For being your hero?"

She smiled. "For the colonel, actually. I think killing him would have, well, changed me, made me into my enemy. I guess that's what Sixto was trying to tell me all along. I'm glad I didn't do it."

"Even though he seems to have gotten off relatively unscathed?"

She nodded.

"What about you, Zaria? What are your plans, now that the treaty has been signed?"

"I don't know. I just want to enjoy my baby for a while." She leaned back with her tea. "It feels odd. My life has never been like this before. No secret meetings. No plotting behind the scenes. It could get boring." She smiled. "I could get used to boring."

"You won't have to, I'm sure." He drank his tea.

During the talks, the major had proven himself a skilled diplomat. He had expertly attended to the interests of Palmarans, without betraying those of his own government. His tireless behind-the-scenes meetings and discussions had helped to foster trust among the negotiators, and his skills had not gone unnoticed. Surely, the Peacekeepers would find him a post where his diplomatic skills could be put to use.

After another sip, he put down the cup. "I'm leaving."

She was sorry but had half expected it. "I'll miss you. Where are they sending you?"

"No, you misunderstand. I'm not leaving Palmares. I'm leaving the Peacekeepers."

"But why? You could have a promotion and the posting of your choice if you stay in the Forces."

"I like it here. I don't want to leave."

"But what will you do here?"

He glanced at her large belly and looked away quickly. "I don't know exactly. A lot of jobs will be created by the new treaty. Replacing the quilidon in the quarries is a big task. More people will come. There will be more commercial opportunities. I'm sure something will come up for a man of my talents." He grinned.

Zaria grinned back. "You're welcome to stay here. With me."

"Here?"

"Yes. I think Sixto would want it."

His eyes held hers. "Thank you. I'd like that."

No, thought Zaria, things will never be the same again, but they might be all right.

ABOUT THE AUTHOR

Zainab's other book-length publications include the sci fi novel *Resistance* and the non fiction works *Wielding the Force: The Science of Social Justice* and *Ways of Wielding: 13 Exercises in Collective Care and Effectiveness.*

Zainab Amadahy is based in peri-apocalyptic Toronto where she is challenged to balance her time as a novelist, non-fic writer, lyricist, screenwriter, educator and mom to three grown sons as well as a male cat. Check her out at http://www.swallowsongs.com/. She loves to engage with readers and you'll find plenty of freebies on the site.

Made in the USA
Columbia, SC
04 September 2017